NAILING THE SINGLE DAD
LIPSTICK AND LEAD 2.0

SYLVIA MCDANIEL

Copyright
Copyright © 2019 Sylvia McDaniel
Published by Virtual Bookseller, LLC
All Rights Reserved
Cover Art by Dar Albert
Edited by Tina Winograd
ebook ISBN 978-1-950858-12-5
Paperback 978-1-950858-13-2

No part of this book may be reproduced, downloaded, transmitted, decompiled, reverse engineered, stored in or introduced to any information storage and retrieval system, in any form, whether electronic or mechanical without the author's written permission. Scanning, uploading or distribution of this book via the Internet or any other means without permission is prohibited.

Please purchase only authorized electronic versions, and do not participate in, or encourage pirated electronic versions.

The Heat is On

My pet name for him is Detective Baby Daddy. Why so harsh, you ask? Because Antonio Marino represents everything I detest in a guy. Unfortunately, we're both after the same criminal. Normally, that wouldn't bother me since I always get my man, but Antonio's boss has ordered us to work together or go to jail. Now I'm wondering who I'll take down in handcuffs first-- Detective Baby Daddy or the trafficking scumbag Torres.

If you ask me, she's a bounty hunter with a chip on her shoulder the size of Texas and a bad attitude to match. You'd think Katherine McKenzie and I hate each other, but I think all this fire and spark between us is a way to resist a building attraction. God help both of us. And now, my boss has instructed me to work with her...or else. Of all the damn luck.

If you'd like to learn about my new releases before anyone else, sign up for my new book alerts.

CHAPTER 1

A month after having her appendix removed, Katherine was once again hunting bounties. This one felt personal. This one was a man who they first issued bail for a year ago, and now once again, he'd skipped out on his hearing.

Why Mateo wasn't locked up somewhere, she didn't know, but Jennifer worked on his case before, and now, she would bring him in to justice. This time, he might no longer be able to make babies when she finished with him.

She'd castrate his balls herself to keep this man from harming anyone else. First, he decided the world needed as many little Torres children as possible and impregnated at least five young girls. But then he made the mistake of touching someone under the age of sixteen and her parents filed charges.

Tonight, Shaggy told her he learned women hanging out at the Silverado Bar had been slipped a roofie and woke up knowing they had sex, but unable to remember anything. At least three people had been given the drug.

Someone needed to teach this asshole a lesson on not messing with women. And she was the right person for the job.

Against her better judgement, Katherine dressed in a tight

pink outfit that clung to her curves, her breasts bubbling over the top and heels that made her legs appear long. The dress barely covered her bottom, and she knew she would never have worn the spandex out of the house, except the outfit made the perfect bait.

Standing in the dark bar, she gazed at the men in the place, thinking she was glad she never had gotten into this scene.

Already three men received a mean enough glare they backed away. There was only one man she was interested in tonight, and so far, there was no sign of him.

Leaning her back against the bar, she held a drink in her hand for decoration.

For a quick second, she turned and checked her phone. Shaggy sat outside in his car, waiting to tell her he was on his way in. The plan was she would seduce him into agreeing to leave with her. Once she had him in the parking lot, baby daddy would be hers.

When she whirled around, there stood her worst nightmare. The handsome Detective Dickhead, Antonio Marino.

"What the hell are you doing here?" Antonio asked, glaring at her as he walked to her side.

She smiled. "Detective Dickhead, why I'm only after what every girl comes here to do. Looking for a hook up."

The man scanned her dress. "Bounty hunter slut, you certainly wore the right disguise tonight. Who are you after?"

The man's words made her want his balls as she stared at him. "Don't interfere in my arrest."

"No, honey, you don't get to arrest them. I do. All you do is nab a man and haul his ass to jail."

"Wouldn't I love to haul your ass to the pokie," she said. "Now go away, I'm working."

"In that skin-tight dress, where did you hide your gun?"

"Wouldn't you like to know. Now go."

The music began to blare in the bar and couples got up to

dance while Katherine stood there and swayed to the beat trying to act like she was alone.

"Do you tango?"

In surprise, her head swiveled to the detective who continued to stand by her side.

"Yes," she said. "Do you?"

"Yes," he replied.

"Of course, you do. That's how you landed your first woman and became a baby daddy."

"Someday, when we're not working, you need to explain to me why you think I'm a baby daddy."

"Why should I? You know the truth. Don't need an explanation from me," she said, her voice filling with the anger that consumed her whenever she thought about a man impregnating a woman and leaving her. Then she saw her prey. "Now bug off. My bounty just walked in the door."

The detective looked out at the crowd. "Oh, hell no, he's mine."

"First one who gets him, keeps him."

With a quick glare at Antonio, she began to walk toward Mateo Torres, a determined step in her six-inch heels. The man was alone and when he saw her, he grinned. "Chica, you're looking hot tonight."

"You're the first man who's walked through the door that I got all flushed when I looked at you."

He took her arm. "Would you like to dance?"

"Of course," she said. They moved to the floor where they begin to salsa. A great dancer with all the right moves both on and off the dance floor, but then why wouldn't he be. Obviously, he was well versed in the art of seduction.

Only this time, it would not end with him being the winner, but her. After the song ended, he leaned forward and said, "Let's grab a drink."

"Sure," she said, hoping to somehow convince him to go with her. Once outside, he would be hers. "Or we could leave now."

"You are caliente."

Grabbing her hand, he dragged her toward the other end of the bar away from the detective. A shiver of revulsion spiraled through her at his touch. When they reached the bar stool, he ordered two drinks and pulled her between his legs.

"You are one hot puta in that pink dress." His finger trailed along the top of her shoulder, letting them dip down toward her breasts. If the man touched the girls, she would have knocked him into next week. As for calling her a whore, later tonight, he would be singing soprano for that comment.

"What's your name?"

"Cissy," she said.

"I'm having a little party at my house. Just me and a few friends. Would you like to come?"

She would agree to just about anything until they got out the door, then her taser and cuffs would secure him. "Sure."

"Here's your drink," he said. "Now be a good girl and drink it all up."

No way she was going to sip that alcohol. Maybe it was clean, but what if he put a roofie in there? Somehow she had to toss it. His attention turned to across the room, and she set the glass on the bar. Quickly, she switched them when he wasn't looking.

"Shit," he said, glancing at her wildly. "Honey, I've got to go."

"No," she said. "We were just getting into each other."

"There's a cop over there and I have some outstanding traffic tickets."

Outstanding traffic tickets her ass. More like he skipped out on his bail, and she was here to haul him in. No way was he going to get away.

"Let me walk you outside," she said, thinking with Shaggy's help, they could take him down.

Two Dallas police officers walked in the door, and he

smiled. "No, beautiful, you stay here. The place is about to go dark."

The lights went out. Pushed off his lap, she barely kept from landing on her ass with her heels wobbling in the darkness.

"Don't move," someone shouted. People around her screamed and she felt a hand wrap around her wrist and steady her.

"Shit," she said, reaching out for Mateo, but he was already gone.

The hand yanked her in close. "Don't move."

Moments later, the lights came on, and she was face to face with Detective Dickhead.

"He recognized you," she spat.

"Do you always get so chummy with the suspect."

"It's called a disguise and as soon as I had him outside, he would have been mine," she yelled.

"I was trying to protect you," he screamed back at her.

After that comment, she didn't hold back and punched him on the arm. "Who said I need your protection."

As she went to hit him again, he blocked her punch. "Stay out of my investigation."

"I've been here way longer you. Don't mess with me."

"Yes, dressed like a high-class hooker."

As his voice echoed throughout the room, they realized the music had stopped. Everyone stood gazing at them.

The two police officers slowly walked over to them. "Come on you two, you're going downtown."

"Look in my pocket, I'm a detective," he told them.

"Don't care," one officer said. "After the scene you two have made here, the owner asked us to remove you."

"Nothing started until after you arrived," Katherine said.

They stared at one another and her urge to haul off and smack him was almost too much.

"Mateo Torres is my bounty."

"And he's my arrest," Detective Dickhead said.

The officers looked at the two of them. "The whole club is listening. It would be best if you both shut up and came downtown with us."

"I'm not going," she said.

"Enough." The officer grabbed her wrist, pulled it behind her and slapped the plastic ties around her skin. "No more arguing, let's go."

"What about him? Doesn't he get cuffed?"

"He's coming along and doesn't have a smart mouth."

"These cuffs aren't going to shut me up," she told the patrol man.

The officer leaned in close. "The boss has plans for the both of you. Now be nice and let's go."

As they walked out of the club, the crowd booed the police, thinking they were being arrested. This might work to her advantage. Being hauled out like she was going to jail, she could come back and look for Mateo again.

But more likely Detective Dickhead and the Dallas Police Department had frightened him away from the Silverado Bar, and now she would need to start over in trying to locate her bounty without the handsome baby daddy interfering.

CHAPTER 2

*A*ntonio knew being hauled in to speak to his boss couldn't be good. Now the two of them stood before Kevin Harris, captain of the Dallas police detectives, and from the grimace on the man's face, something was up.

His cramped office held few photos, yet the wall was filled with his awards for exemplary police service. Outside, the noise of a busy precinct filtered into the space.

"Sit down," he commanded like a drill sergeant.

The officer undid the handcuffs from Katherine's wrists, and she glared at him, curled her lip and stuck her tongue out. The patrolman only smiled and walked out the door, shaking his head.

The woman needed to learn when to act like an adult, rather than a brat.

"Tonight, you interfered in an ongoing investigation."

"No, I was going after a bounty who missed his court date. Since our agency holds the bond, I have every right to bring him in."

The man's face turned red. "You interfered in an investigation. Mateo Torres is suspected of human trafficking. Underage young girls to be precise."

A knock at the door startled them as a man in a suit, looking like a Fed, entered. Oh, shit, he recognized his type as a shiver went through Antonio. FBI.

Katherine's mouth dropped open, and she shook her head. "That asshole."

The woman's potty talk would fit into any police station.

"Meet Special Agent Chad White with the bureau."

The man pulled a chair to where he could face them and sank onto it, placing his elbows on his knees as he leaned toward them.

"Mateo Torres is part of a gang stealing young women and shipping them to the brothels of Mexico. All are underage. Tonight, we were waiting for him, but you two interfered."

"Miss McKenzie, you grabbed his attention, so now we want you to work with us to help secure him. Detective Marino, you will assist her. Our men will be feeding you all the information we can."

"No, I'm not buying any of this," Katherine said, shaking her head. "Mateo just wants to impregnate as many women as possible. Pregnant women are not sent to a brothel."

The men laughed and the agent stared at her like she was green as grass and dumber than a box of rocks. In some ways, she really could be considered a rookie. "The pregnant girls are the lucky ones."

"What about the underage girl? He's accused of statutory rape."

"We think she escaped, and her parents insisted on filing charges. She's terrified because she knows he will kill her before he lets her talk, so we've placed her and her family in hiding until we catch him."

Antonio hated investigations like this one. Already his ten-year-old daughter's interest in boys scared him and this only

NAILING THE SINGLE DAD

reminded him of the dangers she would one day face. He'd kill any man or boy who touched his daughter against her will or with her permission if she was underage.

He would protect Emma at any cost. And he pitied the man who tested him.

Katherine glanced at Antonio. "I don't need Detective D-- Marino. I work alone or with the other women in our agency."

The FBI agent raised his brows and his boss snapped. "You'll work with my detective or you'll lose your license. Do you understand?"

"What? You can't take away my license."

"One phone call is all it would take for your career to be over. And you could be looking at some jail time for disobeying to render help to a public official. Are we clear?"

The woman's bottom lip curled in a snarl that almost had Antonio laughing, yet this investigation would be hell. Hell because Katherine would make his life miserable until the case was resolved.

Why the woman hated him so much, he didn't know. Why she called him Detective Baby Daddy, he didn't understand. Before now, he let her childish behavior ride, but soon, very soon, he was going to confront her about the name-calling. It was the reason he started retaliating with *bounty hunter slut*.

Yes, two adults using childish name-calling that if he caught his daughter saying such things, he would punish her. But after the way Katherine treated him, it felt good to get at least a little payback.

"Detective, are we clear? You're going to work closely with Miss McKenzie."

Inside, he was screaming no but declining would only get him demoted or fired or even worse—put back on patrol. "Yes, sir."

"Now that we've gotten that settled. Agent White, how do you want them to help you?"

He grinned. "Miss McKenzie, you did very well this evening

attracting our perp. We'll be tracking him and as soon as we locate him, we will place you to cross his path again. In the meantime, be on the lookout for Mr. Torres."

The agent stood and so did his boss, letting him know they were being dismissed.

Together, they pushed back their chairs and walked out the door. Once they were out of ear shot, she turned to him. "Detective Dickhead, it will be a cold day in hell before I ever cooperate with you. Don't even think about us working together."

"I'll be sure to tell my captain, so he can put your ass in jail."

"You'd do that, wouldn't you," she said.

"Damn right, I would. Because then I wouldn't have to work with you."

Antonio turned and strode away before he called out, "My office in the morning, nine o'clock sharp."

CHAPTER 3

The next morning when Katherine walked in the door of the Lipstick and Lead agency it was very quiet except for the sound of someone retching.

Gina stood outside the bathroom, her ear next to the door. Brittany beside her, frowning, watching her and Shaggy leaned against the wall, his face wearing a grimace, shaking his head.

"What is going on?" Katherine said, gazing at them. She had a meeting, and she'd dropped by the office to pick up her file on Mateo before going to see Detective Dickhead.

Gina motioned for her to be quiet.

Brittany walked over to her side and whispered. "Jennifer is in the bathroom throwing up and Gina is certain she's pregnant."

"So you're all standing out here listening to her retch?" Katherine shook her head. "Sometimes I'm amazed at the nosiness of people. Did anyone think to ask her if she was all right? It could be a stomach virus."

This was the problem with getting married. For the first nine months, people watched your belly, waiting for the announcement a bun resided in the oven.

"This is the second morning in a row."

"Still doesn't prove she's expecting," Katherine said. "Would you want everyone out here speculating whether you are pregnant if you were throwing up in the bathroom? Sometimes family can be monsters," she said as she hurried into her office and retrieved the file.

When she came back out, they all remained in their designated positions like toy soldiers. Katherine said loudly, "Don't you people have something better to do than speculate she's pregnant?"

Just then Jennifer yanked open the bathroom door and stood gazing at the crowd, looking pale, wiping her hands on a paper towel. "Were you guys listening to me?"

"Are you pregnant?" Katherine asked.

"No, I don't think so," Jennifer said. "Something I ate last night disagreed with me."

The whole office was nosy, certain the announcement of Baby Lopez was on the way.

"Problem solved. Go back to work everyone, crisis averted," Katherine said.

Staring at Katherine, Jennifer said perplexed, "Crisis averted?"

"Don't get your panties in a twist, it's just an expression. And I wasn't the one standing out here with my ears pinned to the door listening to you puke," she said, stuffing her file folder in her bag. She needed to get on the road, so she wouldn't be late.

"What? Who was listening?"

If she said Gina's name, the fight would be on. Time to bow out of this fracas. "Do your own investigating. I've got to go or I'll be late."

"Where are you going?" Jennifer asked.

"I've got a meeting with Detective Dickhead against my better judgement," she said.

Blocking the bathroom door, Jennifer, glared at them. "Even you, Shaggy?"

"Been standing here the entire time. All I want to do is wash my hands," he said.

A swirl of a neon yellow spandex skirt and Gina headed toward the kitchen. "Merlin is calling me."

"What? I don't hear that cat?" Jennifer called.

"Only I can hear his special meow," she said and disappeared behind the door.

"I'm not pregnant," Jennifer yelled as Katherine walked out the door and ran smack into her Uncle Sam.

"Whoa, where are you off to so early this morning? Any luck getting that bad boy Mateo last night?"

Cars whizzed down the street and Katherine didn't want to be late to her meeting. One minor fender bender brought Dallas traffic to a grinding halt where you sat for hours.

"Nope, but that's where I'm headed to now. Now we've got the Feds involved in trying to catch him."

Her uncle smiled. "Good. He'll be caught soon."

"Gotta go," she called as she raced down the steps to her car.

Why was he so certain the FBI could do a better job than the Dallas police department and her? Frankly, the federal and state agencies were too bogged down in red tape, where she could bring him without giving him his Maranda rights or anything else.

And if the man was lucky, he'd arrive with his balls intact.

CHAPTER 4

She was late. Or maybe she decided she preferred jail to working with him, which would be even better. Of all the people in the world, why had his boss assigned him this spitfire? Sure, he was aiming for department head and one of the things they examined was his ability to work with anyone.

Including a stubborn woman bounty hunter with a chip on her shoulder the size of Mount Rushmore.

This morning, he arrived early to pull the records on Mateo Torres, whose rap sheet looked more like a phone book. From the time he was a young man who joined a gang, to his latest legal battle, statutory rape of a minor. Every father's nightmare.

Looking at the mug shot, he wondered what Katherine had on him.

A knock on his door and then she walked through. "Sorry, I'm late, but some idiot decided to race through-traffic and clipped two cars, causing a major accident on 635."

Traffic was always an excuse in Dallas, and she should have left earlier.

"Leaving earlier usually avoids these problems."

Watching her, she tensed, and he realized that probably wasn't a good way to start them out working together, but he expected her to be on time. Tardiness always irritated him.

"I left at seven, but I went by the office to pick up our file on this asshole, thinking that would be helpful. Next time, I'll make certain I'm here on time without the information."

What could he say? They needed to compare notes and learn where they stood. The Lipstick and Lead agency probably had as much info on the perp as he did.

"Let's get to work," he said. "Here is his rap sheet and all the data on him, including his home address."

Dragging the paperwork closer, she glanced through the documents.

"He won't be there," she said. "Shaggy and Jennifer went there last week and it's bogus. His aunt lives there, and she said he's never even stayed the night."

Typical and to be expected. True criminals used more addresses and aliases, always looking for a way to keep law enforcement officials at bay.

"We checked his bank account and let's just say he's dealing with cash only. Knows the system is after him, so not a single debit card transaction," she said, looking through the folder. "Did you run his license plate through the toll booths to see if he's been on the highway?"

How did she know about that? Not many people understood that every time they went through a toll booth the police could track them. Of course, most people didn't need to worry about being tracked.

"Yes, and nothing. He's not driving on major toll roads."

"What about downtown cameras? Has your facial recognition software seen him?"

Damn, she knew her stuff and all the tricks. "No."

The man was very adept at hiding out. As a juvenile offender, he grew up with law enforcement cataloging his every crime and learned how to work the system.

"What about the list of women who are supposedly carrying his child and receiving welfare. Did anyone interrogate them or verify these babies are truly his."

Antonio leaned back in his chair. It seemed like such a devious plot, and yet, it would be taking care of unborn children. He'd seen starving children before, and he was glad they received food stamps.

"I detest this idea," he said.

She frowned at him. "Me too. But what if it's true?"

"Then he needs to be found and stopped. Let's make a list of the girls and go see them."

The pregnant women would be receiving free healthcare and help with their pregnancy, but for the bastard to take that small pittance of a check from the welfare they received made Antonio's blood turn cold. The sooner they caught this guy, the better for everyone.

"Is there anyone else who is close to him?"

"A brother and sister," he told her, thinking for the first time since they met, she seemed to be working with him. He liked the way she acted, serious about putting a stop to this criminal.

"I've added them to the list," she said. "What about old gang members. Friends. Does he have any?"

Antonio laughed. "If you were friends, you would realize how he treated women and would refuse to let any woman you care about go near him."

"True," she said. "If you knew. What if he pretends to be a choir boy in front of his buddies?"

"No, I'm not buying the choir boy act," he said. "For one thing, in these types of gangs, you want to be seen as macho. Manly. A stud muffin with tattoos and piercings."

The woman rolled her eyes. "That's with any man," she said in a low voice.

A grin spread across his face. "Would you date a wimp?"

The way she stopped going through her paperwork and glared at him was staggering.

"No, I don't date."

That was a shocker. Something he didn't know if he believed.

"What do you mean you don't date? After the way you acted in the club last night, did you and your boyfriend fight?"

That dress she wore had awakened places of his body long forgotten. It fit her curves like a glove, and as a man, it left an impact.

Her big brown eyes oozed irritation.

"My one and only date ended when the boy who asked me to the prom tried something inappropriate and received a black eye. No boy in high school ever had the courage to ask me out again.

"In college, I worked my way through and didn't have time to date. Now, I don't do dating apps, or setups or anything else, so I don't date."

Stunned, Antonio stared at the woman. With her long ebony hair and large eyes with long lashes, she was gorgeous, and men never pursued her? No way, he accepted she didn't date and had to be lying. Then again, with that chip on her shoulder, maybe no man braved getting close to asking her out.

"Let me find you a date," he said.

She glared at him. "Listen to me, I said, I don't do setups."

"You know if you would smile more and knock that chip off your shoulder, I bet guys would come crawling out of the woodwork to date you."

Sitting back, she gazed at him in a way his skin should be burning, her eyes narrowing. "Did I ask for your help?"

Oh, this subject got to her. Like nails against the chalkboard, where you wanted to take out your revolver and shoot the person irritating you. Exactly what he enjoyed doing. Seeing her squirm.

"No, but I'm just that kind of guy. Before this is over, you're going to be dating."

"No, I'm not. Back to business. We have five girls to interview, his brother and sister, and anyone else the Feds give us."

"Oh yeah, I forgot about them."

How could he forget about the FBI since they were the ones who got him in this situation? Without their whining about him and her interfering in their investigation, neither one of them would be sitting here working this case together.

"Let's get started," she said. "This afternoon I have a meeting to attend."

"With your therapist?"

A sarcastic smile spread across her face. "No, but once I receive my degree in counseling, I'll give you a free session. Let's go."

CHAPTER 5

When they pulled up in front of the house, Katherine thought they had the wrong place. The home was stunning. "Are you sure this is the right address?"

"That's what it says on the paperwork."

Since Detective Dickhead insisted they go in his official police business vehicle, they both stepped out of the car. "Wow," she said. "My first ride in an unmarked car. Can I just tell you that car can only be described as a POS?"

"What is a POS?"

"A piece of shit that should be driven to the junk yard."

"Tell the taxpayers, not me," he said on the sidewalk, not paying her much mind.

Yes, the car was definitely not one he would ever buy used. The thing was run into the ground chasing bad guys. The bullet holes gave it aerodynamics.

Walking onto the porch, they both glanced around trying to peer inside before Katherine rang the bell.

"Yes?" a voice said through a speaker.

"Police," Antonio replied. "We need to speak to Isabella Garcia."

"Who?"

"This is the address she put on her paperwork and if we don't talk to her, we will tell the welfare department she is not living here. Does she live here or not?"

After a delay, the door cracked open and a very pregnant woman stood staring at them. "I'm Isabella Garcia. What do you want?"

The young beautiful woman looked like a model except for the belly that protruded from her.

"May we come in?"

The woman pulled back the door farther, and they stepped into the elaborate home.

"Please sit down." She pointed to two chairs and a long golden couch.

Katherine glanced around the room to the open doorways, looking to make certain there were not any hidden places where someone could pop out. As she gazed at the nice furniture and paintings on the wall, she located a second way out of the house.

"Do you know Mateo Torres?"

A flicker of terror showed up in her eyes, and she tried to smile.

"Of course, he's the father of my child."

"Is he here?"

"No, we don't see much of him," she said, gazing about nervously.

The woman sat back against the sofa.

"When's your baby due," Katherine asked envious of the fact she was pregnant. Though she had a hard time with men, she would love to someday have a family of her own.

"Next month. Won't be long now," Isabella said, a slight smile on her face.

There must be so much to prepare for an infant arriving, and she wondered what would happen to this child.

"Are you having a boy or a girl?" Katherine asked, trying to build rapport with the girl before she asked the hard questions, hoping Detective Dickhead would not start with the ones they really needed answers to.

"A boy," she said with a smile, rubbing her hand over her stomach. "He's name will be Dante."

"Is that the name you and Mateo chose?" There were so many little things Katherine wanted to ask, but mostly she had to ask pertinent questions that would reveal her emotions.

The girl grew nervous again, her lips pressed together in a grimace. "No, I picked the name of my son."

Her gaze glanced nervously around the house and Katherine saw the cameras in the corners. They were being watched.

"Do you have any other children?" Katherine asked and noticed Antonio frowned at her.

"No, this one is my first." A smiled crossed her face, and she rubbed her hand on her stomach.

"Babies are so special. Your family must be so excited and helping you prepare a nursery and getting everything ready for his arrival."

A tear welled up in her eye and the girl leaned forward and covered her face with her hands. "They will not speak to me. Papa said we should have waited until we married."

Leaning close to her, Katherine turned her mouth away from the cameras and whispered, "Are you being held here against your will?"

The girl sat up dried her eyes and smiled. "Mateo says he will come see us when he can. But he's so busy working."

"Where does he work?"

The girl shrugged. "I don't know."

Now Katherine didn't know what to believe. One minute, Katherine feared she was being held against her will and the next Isabella acted like this was the only place she could go. If her family wouldn't help her, what choice did she have?

"Four other women are pregnant by him," Detective Marino

said. An unneeded statement that made the young woman clam up. Even if Mateo wasn't the father, his words made the girl look stupid. Men.

The girl hung her head, but she didn't respond. "What other questions?"

Antonio crossed his arms. "One last question. What can you tell me about the stable of women Mateo has working for him in a brothel? Were you one of his girls?"

The woman's face blanched and Katherine knew it was true. She'd been at a brothel and this was not Mateo's child, but some unknown man's. Yet it was clear she wanted to keep her baby.

All the heartache of what would happen to that infant ricocheted like a machine gun through Katherine, leaving her full of holes. Another child left without both parents.

"Miss Garcia, we'll let you go. If you can think of anything else about Mr. Mateo, please contact the police department, and they'll transfer you to Detective D--Marino," she said.

Knowing she almost called him Detective Dickhead to a potential criminal, but at least the girl would have known the truth.

The girl rose from the couch, clearly relieved they were leaving.

Was it because she feared them, or did she fear the people in the house? The sound of footsteps upstairs and suddenly Katherine wondered if there could be other girls here.

"Are there other pregnant women living here?"

The woman's eyes widened, and she shook her head a little too much to be believable. What if all of Mateo's baby mammas were in one location?

At the door, the girl opened it and stood waiting for them to leave, her face appeared almost weary.

"Good luck with your baby," Katherine said, leaning forward, clasping her hand in hers, she placed a business card in the girl's palm. Her eyes widened with fright. "We're here to protect and serve," Katherine said, trying to relay the message to the girl they could help her if she chose to escape.

"Goodbye," she said, closing the door on them.

As they walked down the sidewalk, Katherine couldn't stop herself, she turned and glanced up at the house in time to see a shadow at the window.

"She's not alone. Someone is there with her," she said as they reached the car. "What if it's the other girls?"

The detective looked up. "Maybe, I didn't think about them all being in the same house."

"When we were saying goodbye, I gave her my card."

"How did you do that?"

"At the door, when I clasped her hands in mine. She was shaking. Terrified. What if she is just the incubator for that child?"

"Could be. I've seen stranger things," he said, climbing into the car.

With one last glance at the house, Katherine crawled into the vehicle. For some reason, she wanted to run back into the house and grab the young woman and rush her out. Seeing that camera while they spoke left an eerie feeling of big brother watching. A sense of secrecy seemed to ebb from the house.

"Detective Dickhead, I think Isabella is being held against her will. In fact, I'm willing to bet going on a date with some unknown creepy guy, she's a hostage. I'm hoping she'll call me when she gets a chance."

Antonio turned and gazed at her. "You've got yourself a bet. Because she is being held against her will. While you were talking babies with her, she passed me this note."

Whirling toward him, Katherine took the piece of paper from his hands.

Please help me. I can't leave, and they are going to make me give my baby away.

"So I won. You should have shared this before we made this bet. It made you the loser."

"Maybe. What kind of men do you like?" Antonio asked as they backed out of the drive.

"I don't. And I'm not going on a date. No need, I won."

"Oh, you like women then?"

"No, I don't."

She gritted her teeth, wishing he would stop thinking of trying to set her up. Men found her bossy and exasperating. "How are we going to get her out?"

The man frowned. "Don't know yet, but I'm working on an idea."

"Good, at least that will keep you busy rather than finding me a date."

He chuckled. "Don't worry, this brain has room for both."

CHAPTER 6

Katherine took a seat and stared at the girls in her group. As a part of her degree program, she had to lead a counseling group. She chose young girls who faced the same problem she had growing up. A missing parent.

While her counselor kept telling her to tone down her reactions to people, she thought that made her honest and sincere and helped her get along with the preteens.

This way, they didn't think of her as the older woman who told them what to do. Six young ladies between the ages of nine and twelve met once a week. One just happened to be Detective Dickhead's daughter. Sadly, he didn't realize she was the intern counselor in his daughter's group.

In fact, he'd met Pat Brindle, the psychotherapist, but not her, in this setting. And what Antonio didn't understand was the very reason she called him Detective Baby Daddy or Detective Dickhead. For the way he treated his daughter.

"How is everyone this afternoon? Good day at school?"

Sarah tensed. "Why do kids with fathers rub it in that yours is not there? At lunch today, I smacked this fat kid Jeff because he told me if I wasn't so ugly, my father wouldn't have left."

The urge to kick young Jeff's behind was strong, but as a counselor that would be frowned upon.

Pat glanced at her while she listened to the young girl, hearing the pain in her voice and knowing how she felt. In junior high, Katherine had beat the crap out of some kid for saying her father didn't love her, and she was the reason he moved on. Three suspension days later, she realized he was probably right when her father never showed up for their weekend together.

"What a mean thing to say. Do you think you're ugly?"

The girl sighed. "None of the boys think I'm pretty in school and daddy's gone. Maybe I am. Do you think he left because of me?"

"Of course not."

The other girls started shaking their heads and Katherine felt happy to witness them rallying around their friend. "Don't listen to Jeff," Emma said. "The kids tease him for being overweight. He's trying to make you feel bad about yourself, since he feels bad."

Smart kid. She was always impressed with Emma, but she wondered how Detective Dickhead had such a great daughter. Everyone arrived here with a deadbeat father or mother. But the worst part, she knew Emma's deadbeat dad.

"Have any of you read the story of the ugly duckling?" Katherine asked. Most of them nodded. One or two did not.

"Your homework assignment is to read the book. Because you girls are at that stage in your life where you're changing from a child to a young woman. You're changing from a duckling to a swan, just like in the book."

A frown crossed Emma's face. "Not everyone turns out beautiful. Some people will never be pretty on the outside."

"Very true," Katherine said, thinking this kid was way too smart. "Beauty is not just about how you appear. It's what's on the inside and how you treat others that makes you beautiful."

For a moment, she paused to make sure they understood. "If you're the prettiest girl in school, but you treat people less fortunate either mean or ugly, you don't have true beauty. Meanness will make people dislike you more than anything. If Jeff had said something kind to Sarah how would we all be feeling about him now?"

The girls smiled.

"Let's kick his butt," Jane said, a ten-year-old who had a history of fighting at school. "So, I would be ugly if tomorrow I go in and whoop Jeff's ass?"

Pat gave Katherine a glance that was a warning. They had worked together enough to know the signals.

"If you saw an ugly duckling and a beautiful swan fighting, what would you think? On the outside, you're a beautiful young girl, but brawling will get you in trouble. Because of the way Jeff treated Sarah how many like this boy less?"

Several raised their hands.

This child always made her work. Somehow she had to show them that reacting to other children with violence was not the key to making their life better.

"I would be getting revenge for my friend."

"And that would be your third fight. You would be looking at suspension. What if Jeff is acting out because he thinks no one likes him? Sometimes when people are hurting, they don't say the nicest things."

Jane sighed. "My mother said if I got kicked out of school again, she would put me in a girl's home."

Dear Lord, that was not what this girl needed.

"Who else had problems at home or school?"

Laura sat quietly not saying a word. Of all the children, Katherine worried about this child the most. Her mother and father had recently separated, and she was not taking the breakup of the family well.

"Laura, you're awfully quiet," she said, trying to bring the girl out of her shell. "How was your day?"

"Terrible," she said. "Do I have to go home?"

That landed like a hand grenade right into Katherine's heart. No child had ever said that to her.

"You could come stay with me," Emma told her quietly.

"What's going on, Laura."

At nine years of age, the child appeared lost. "My mother has a boyfriend."

The other girls laughed. "Did he spend the night?" Jane asked. "Wait until you wake up and find him in his underwear in the kitchen making coffee."

Dear God, these kids went through things she never experienced.

"Not yet. I kept hoping my daddy would come home," she said softly. "At his house last weekend, my sister found some lady's clothes in a drawer."

While the parents were moving on, the children still wanted to salvage the family and it didn't sound like it could be saved. All kids no matter what, wanted their parents back together. Unless they were older and understood the reasons for the divorce.

"Next he'll want you to meet her," a little blonde-haired girl said.

The clock ticked toward the end of the hour and several she needed to hear from. Plus, she still had to address the not going home portion of Laura's comment.

"Laura, your mother loves you. You're upset because your father left, but what if you didn't return? How would your mother feel?"

The child shrugged like she wasn't quite certain. "But if she'd been nicer to daddy, he would have stayed."

"No, you don't know if that was the problem," Katherine told her, thinking she had grown up believing her mother was at fault for years. Now she realized the truth regarding her own family.

So many of these kids wouldn't realize the reality about their parents until they were in their twenties or later or ever.

"Moms and dads don't always let us witness what the real problem between them is. They try to protect their children."

"No," Sandra said. "My mother tells everyone my father is a lying dirt bag."

If Katherine could speak her opinion, she would agree with her mother. Sandra's mother was better off without the lying dirt bag.

"We've only got five minutes left. Does anyone else want to talk?"

Emma smiled at her. "Miss Katherine, you look very nice today. My daddy is picking me up later. You should come outside and meet him."

And have him learn she was his daughter's counselor, and that she knew all his secrets, the reason she called him Detective Baby Daddy. Oh, no. Not no, but hell no. Emma sent flowers to her in the hospital and everyone believed they came from Detective Dickhead.

The card even read from Antonio, but what Emma didn't realize was they didn't like each other and it was something she could never know.

"All right, girls, it's time. Stand and give one another a hug and repeat after me. 'We are strong young ladies. With help, we can face anything. With love, we will conquer our world.' See you next week," she told them.

After the girls filed out of the room, Pat turned to her and smiled. "Well, they were full of energy today. I thought you handled Sarah and Jane extremely well. Especially when you told Jane that would be her third suspension. As for Laura, I'm concerned about her."

Katherine was worried about the young girl as well. When a child didn't want to go home, there was a problem. Home should be their place of safety and security.

"Me too," Katherine said. "When she said she didn't want to go home, I didn't know what to say."

"You reminded her that her mother loves her. That was excellent. Though I wish her mother would not bring a boyfriend over until the children are ready."

Absolutely, but the woman seemed intent on finding her next husband.

"Agree, but I doubt that's going to happen," she said with a sigh.

"Probably not," Pat said. "See you next week. Good work this afternoon."

"Thanks," Katherine said hanging back. She didn't want Detective Baby Daddy to be standing outside waiting for his daughter, so she always allowed extra time. Plus, it gave her time to write up her notes.

CHAPTER 7

*A*ntonio loved his adopted daughter more than he ever thought possible. When he married her mother, he never dreamed he would fall in love with the child, but she captured his heart.

Not long after he and Sheila tied the knot, he learned about her deadbeat sperm donor. The thought of what this man had done to Emma had him asking Sheila if he could make her his daughter.

When she turned five, they went through the process of him adopting Emma, and since then, she bore his name. Though she didn't come from his DNA, she was the daughter of his heart, his choice, and now no one could claim her. After Sheila died in the line of duty, they helped one another get through the loss of their loved one.

Now that Emma had lost both parents, he decided it would be good to help her deal with any remaining issues of her father's abandonment and her mother's violent death. So once a week she attended a group counseling session.

Emma opened the car door and bounced inside and gave him a hug. Those hugs were the best.

"So how was group today?"

"Daddy, we are so blessed. Yes, we both miss momma and as the teacher likes to call them baby daddies, I recognize how fortunate I am to have you."

As he backed out of the parking lot, he glanced at the building where the police psychotherapist recommended he take Emma. What his daughter didn't realize was that without her there, he would have been so alone when he lost Sheila.

"You know I love you baby girl," he said.

"Yes, I do, but it still hurts my own father would walk away and leave me and mother."

"Understand and that's why you're going to the counselor."

While he knew she loved him, he understood the older she got, the more she would resent her father for turning his back on the two of them.

It was hard for Antonio to fathom. How did you abandon your child? For years, he and Sheila tried to conceive a baby, hoping they would expand their family, but it wasn't meant to be. Still, he had his daughter.

And when his wife died, she'd taken part of his heart with her. Though sometimes Emma told him he needed to find someone else, he just couldn't. What if they didn't love Emma the way he loved her? What about the house? Nothing had changed since the day Sheila had been shot.

Sure, he got lonely. But his soul seemed empty, and he didn't know if anyone could ever fill it again. Learning his wife had been gunned down doing her job ate at him like a cancer.

As he drove through traffic toward their home, Emma rambled on about the session. While he was sorry **it** was necessary for her to attend, he enjoyed their time together afterward, talking about what she learned.

"Today there was a girl in there whose mother and father split up two months ago. Her mother has a boyfriend and he spent the night. Poor Laura, she didn't want to go home."

These were the kinds of things he dealt with when he was a patrolman working the street. To learn his kid was hearing these types of stories somewhat bothered him.

"Does it upset you when you hear about kids who are going through this?"

She laughed. "Are you kidding me. I thank God my mother found a good man who wanted both of us. Who became my father in ways my biological dad obviously could not. I'm probably the luckiest girl in the class."

"Even though you lost your parents."

"You're my parent. You're my father," she said.

His heart swelled with love, and as much as he missed his wife, he was lucky he had a child who reminded him so much of her. At first, it hurt to look at Emma and see Sheila sitting there. After a while, he felt blessed Sheila had entrusted him with the person she loved so very much.

Emma didn't know, but her mother made several videos for her. When she was older, he was to give them to her. One when she went away to college and the other when she married. All of these she prepared after she joined the force, just in case. Though she never believed she would die doing her job.

Now, he couldn't think about those times. Once Emma left, he would be truly alone. He loved being a detective, but he loved coming home to Emma and listening to how her day went.

"Everything was all right at school?"

"Oh, yeah. The usual homework and I have to read The Ugly Duckling."

"Didn't your mother read that to you when you were little?"

"Yes, but it's our assignment for next week and I want to experience the story again."

Like the ugly duckling, his daughter was growing from a child into a budding young woman. Though he dreaded the day he would have to start dealing with her maturing body.

Already changes were beginning, and he feared what that

would mean for him and for Emma. That might be a job he would ask his sister to tackle. Then again, if he didn't tell her about her monthly cycle and the reproduction of life, she would never come to him when she had questions.

That would be a time for him to suck up being a single father and learn to deal with what women went through each month.

"How do you feel about stopping and getting pizza tonight?"

The memory of the young woman he interviewed with Katherine left a pain gripping his chest. He'd kill any man who touched his daughter. He glanced at the beautiful girl and knew the coming teenage years were going to be difficult. Yet he would protect her with his life.

"At Ramono's?" she asked excited.

"Is that what you want?" he said.

"You really need a wife."

"What brought that on?" he asked a certain dark-haired woman he often fought with coming to mind.

"Because you're sweet and kind. Not like so many of the men I learn about in this class. The teacher is single."

Dear God, Emma was trying to set him up.

"No," he said quickly. "Not after losing your mother."

Still, a bounty hunter with a sassy mouth refused to get out of his brain. The woman was as mean as a rattlesnake. Why in the world would he be attracted to her?

Because she was different.

CHAPTER 8

The next day, Katherine and Antonio sat outside the house where Isabella lived and watched the different cars that came and went, writing down the license plates and trying to decide if now was the time to take the girl or wait.

"Did the brother and sister speak to you?"

"No, they refused to answer any questions and said they wanted nothing to do with their brother."

"That's convenient," she said.

Sitting here just watching was so boring.

"Five vehicles within three hours," she said. "These people either have lots of company or something's going on inside that house."

"Why would they make her give up the baby?"

"So she can be sent to work in the brothel."

"What will they do with the child? They must be doing something with the baby, otherwise, as cruel as it sounds, I'd think they'd force her to have an abortion."

When it came to babies and children, Katherine was a softie, and the thought of a mother being forced to abandon a child had her blood pumping through her tight chest.

None of this made sense to her. If they wanted her for the sex trade, why wouldn't she be on birth control pills or condoms? Especially to prevent the spread of HIV. Years ago, prostitutes had no choice, but now there were so many ways to keep from having an unwanted pregnancy.

"Mexico is a Catholic country. Abortions are illegal and go against the laws of the church. Even here in America, it's become difficult. Still, people like this don't care about rules. There has to be some kind of monetary value."

Katherine sat in the hot Texas sun watching a house where she knew criminal activities occurred, trying to figure out what to do next.

"Black-market adoptions," she said out loud. "How much money is involved in a system where parents who can't adopt a baby any other way seek out the black market."

Was she onto something here? Could Mateo be selling these children?

Antonio frowned, his dark brows drawing together as he turned to stare at her. "A Caucasian child is around thirty-five thousand dollars. All other babies run about twenty thousand."

"So currently we know of five girls who are pregnant. You're looking at more than a hundred grand. What if there are more?"

Shaking his head, Antonio said, "No. Just no."

"How did we learn about these girls? Someone from the Temporary Assistance for Needy Families office became suspicious. What made them suspect something?"

"They all listed Mateo as the father."

"Yes," she said.

"A smart criminal would not list his name on the application. But why would anyone care how many children he created? It's not against the law to have multiple children."

She nodded. "Why keep the girls' babies? Why not ship them across the border to the brothels? Seems to me, it would cost him a lot of money to keep them together."

Sex trafficking and pregnant women. What did the two have to do with one another? Why were they keeping pregnant women?

"They're all United States citizens," he said, and she could tell he was thinking about the connection.

Sitting in the driver's seat, Antonio tapped his fingers on the steering wheel of the car as they stared at the house.

"Maybe with border security so tight, they don't want the mother and baby becoming separated."

"If they made the mother give up the child, they would not transfer the baby to Mexico. No, that baby is being sold."

"True, but unless they crossed the border illegally, if the girl is on the missing persons list, she would be found right away and returned to her family."

None of this made sense. The FBI was at a loss as to what was going on with these young women who were obviously pregnant. Young, barely eighteen and Mateo was listed as the father on the applications for welfare.

"Come on," she said, getting out of the unmarked car. "We're going to rescue Isabella, and then we're going to learn the truth. The time for sitting and watching is over."

Without waiting for him, she started toward the house. In the background, she heard him call for back up, but she didn't care.

When she knocked on the door, Isabella answered. "Do you want to escape?"

The girl's eyes widened. "They will kill me."

"If you want to leave, come with me, now. We have a place where you can stay. You'll be protected."

She glanced behind her and then walked out the door. "Hurry."

"Don't you want to pack your things?"

Katherine had not thought about her just walking out the door, she expected for her to want her possessions, but this might be safer.

"No, let's go before they realize what's going on."

Stunned, Katherine took the pregnant lady by the arm and tried to hurry her across the street. Antonio stood near the car being vigilant. Though the woman waddled as fast as she could, it was barely a crawl.

As they reached the vehicle door, a man came running out. "Stop. What are doing with my daughter?"

"Is he your father?"

"No, and he has a gun."

Well, that was good to know. She pushed the girl into the car, not wanting to endanger the young woman and her baby even more.

"Sir, leave her alone. She's going with us."

"You're making a mistake," the man said. "Isabella, don't do this."

Tears began to run down the woman's face.

"Go, please go," she said.

Antonio jumped in the car and started the engine.

From across the street, she saw the man pull out a pistol. "Stop or I'll kill her."

"Down in the floorboard," Katherine demanded. "Now."

The woman tried to lie down, her big belly in the way.

A pop, pop sound echoed in the street as Antonio put the car in drive. "What the hell? He's firing at us."

"Get us out of here, Dickhead," Katherine screamed. The man put in another clip. "He's reloading."

Antonio pulled away while the man filled the back of the vehicle with bullets.

"Isabella, are you all right," Katherine called to the girl as Antonio raced down the street.

The young girl didn't respond. Fear gripped her chest as she turned and saw blood in the back seat, her heart leapt into her throat.

"Go! Get us to the hospital. She's been shot."

CHAPTER 9

Chad, the FBI agent, met them at the hospital. "What the hell are you two doing? You were supposed to be watching for Mateo, not rescuing his girlfriend."

Wouldn't it be better to consider their reasons for saving her before he jumped to conclusions they were idiots?

"No, something is not right here. She was petrified," Katherine told him.

"And now she has a bullet in her," he said. "You two mishandled this and now we need to make certain Mateo doesn't recognize you or there is no reason to keep you on the case."

Katherine got up in the agent's face. "This was my case to begin with. I'm trying to catch Mateo and put him behind bars, hopefully forever."

The man shook his head and walked off.

Whenever you pissed the Feds off, things did not go well. They could be yanked off this investigation and suddenly Antonio didn't want that to happen. What if Katherine was right and these babies were being sold on the black market?

For his own peace of mind, he needed to understand and bring a halt to this abomination whatever Mateo had cooked up.

"Well, we certainly handled that one in a positive way that made the agent think well of us."

"Screw the agent. Something is not right. We need to talk to Isabella."

"They're cleaning the bullet wound. It's not bad, but the doctor wants to keep her overnight."

"No way, in hell," she said. "That's all it would take for them to snatch her back again."

"Which means one of us gets to stay the night," Antonio said, thinking of his daughter and how much he didn't like to leave her. Katherine was single. "Tag, you're it. You're on guard duty tonight."

"I figured as much," she said. "Were we wrong?"

For the last hour, he'd been questioning the decision Katherine made to go after Isabella. If they left Isabella alone, would she have been safer?

A bullet grazed her arm, lodging in her upper shoulder. The wound was not life threatening, but the chances of being injured in a shootout was so much worse, not to mention the danger to the baby.

"Don't know the answer. Maybe tonight when you're staying with her, you should find that out. Do some of that woman-to-woman kind of talk. The one where she confesses what this is all about."

She glared at him. Something he said she didn't like. "When are you going to do something in this investigation? I'm the one who decided to move on Isabella while you sat in the car."

"Not fair. Someone had to call for backup."

"Which never arrived," she said.

Partners made decisions together, and she jumped out without discussing the matter with him first. Her recklessness was a problem that endangered them both.

"And what good did that do us? Now we're sitting here in the

ER waiting for her to go to her room, so we can take a statement from her that will not be admissible in court."

"Why wouldn't the information be admissible?"

"Because she's probably under the influence of some drug for the pain."

"She's pregnant. They don't give you the strong painkillers."

"The decision to go to the door should have been made together, not you just jumping out of the car on a whim. It was a reckless move that could have gotten us both killed."

Her body stiffened and her brown eyes shot bullets at him.

"Because of my actions, we saved her. Hopefully she'll talk, and we'll learn some definite answers to what this is all about. Instead of throwing daggers at a dart board. Without my bold move, this investigation would still be going nowhere."

The woman was so stubborn. As detectives, they needed to proceed with caution because if they made Isabella mad, she would turn against them in a heartbeat. Then they would find themselves up to their necks in legal problems.

From the set of her mouth, she wasn't happy with his comments.

"We shouldn't work together. A young woman being pregnant is just another reminder of your past."

What the hell was she referring too. Was she crazy?

"What are you talking about?"

"Detective Baby Daddy--here she comes," Katherine said moving so the stretcher where the girl lay could pass.

The girl moaned, her eyes groggy. "So tired. When are they going to let me rest?"

"We're almost to your room," the attendant told her. "Who are you?"

"Dallas police department," Antonio said flashing his badge. "We're staying with her tonight."

Once they had her settled in a room, Antonio glanced at

Katherine. Should he go off and leave the two of them or arrange for Mrs. Langford to stay with his daughter?

"Go," Katherine said. "You want to get home. But you owe me."

"I knew you couldn't do something out of the goodness of your heart."

"Damn straight," she told him. "Look, you may fool people, but I know who you are. Now go home and play baby daddy."

If he hadn't been in such a hurry to get to Emma, he would have asked her why she was so hostile toward him. Why she insisted on calling him a baby daddy, especially when his daughter was adopted.

CHAPTER 10

Katherine hated hospitals. Lately it felt like she spent more than her fair share of time at one. Yet here she was again. As she glanced at the sleeping Isabella, she wondered about her life.

Though she had yet to awaken, Katherine was glad when Antonio left. This way she could interrogate Isabella without him being around. Maybe she would talk more without a man being present.

The girl moaned in her sleep and Katherine was tempted to pinch her to wake her up.

Suddenly she sat straight up. "Where am I?"

"The hospital," Katherine said touching her on the arm to try to calm her.

"The baby?"

"Is fine," she said, trying to reassure her as she poured her a glass of water. "Do you remember what happened?"

"No," Isabella said. "Oh no, I think I screwed up."

"No," Katherine said and for the next five minutes told her how she arrived here.

The woman frowned and then started to get out of bed. "I need to get out of here."

"Why?"

"This was a mistake and I must go back."

"Stop," Katherine said and the girl looked at her and began to cry. "You sent us a note that said please help me, so we rescued you. If you want to return, say so and I'll take you back. You wrote *I can't leave, and they're going to take my baby away.*"

The girl's big brown eyes filled with tears, and she stared at Katherine. She could see the indecision in the girl's eyes.

"Tell me what's going on and I'll do everything I can to help you."

Leaving must have terrified her and now she was pregnant with no place to go and even a bad situation must look good.

"Can I have some ice cream?"

"Sure." She hit the call button and told the nurse what they needed. Soon a lady appeared at the door with a small cup and spoon.

"Here you go," she said. "Is there anything else?"

"No," Katherine said, wishing the girl would leave, so Isabella might talk.

The pregnant woman dug into the ice cream devouring the sweet cold cream. "They wouldn't let us eat ice cream."

While she tried not to rush the woman, she did her best to act almost uninterested. "Who wouldn't let you have something so good for a baby? Milk is good for babies."

"Yes, but you can also put on too much weight if you consume a lot of high carb foods. They wanted us back working as soon as possible."

"You're pregnant. That baby is taking all the nutrients from your body. You need nutritious food."

The girl smiled. "Do you have kids?"

"No, I'm not married," Katherine said.

"Do you have a boyfriend?"

Part of her didn't want to answer, but she also understood this was a way of Isabella feeling like they had a bond. Maybe she thought Katherine's life was normal, which it wasn't.

"No, no boyfriend."

For a moment, she was silent as she scraped the last of the cup. With a sigh, she placed the empty carton on the tray. "I've been so stupid. I believed everything he said."

"How is that?"

Pulling the covers up around her, she leaned back in the bed.

"Over a year ago, I graduated from high school. My plans were to attend the local community college. Instead, I met Mateo who made me feel so pretty. He treated me special and gained my trust. After we dated for several months, he sat me down and told me all about his dreams. How he wanted to be the richest man in Texas."

Her eyes were distraught, her lips pulled into a grimace as she talked about Mateo. Startled, Katherine realized she had fallen in love with him. Probably still loved him.

The girl took a drink of water and ran her hand over her belly.

"Do you know how attractive that is to a poor young girl? Mateo said he needed my help. He promised to make me his queen. We would live a life of luxury. No need for me to go to college, because he would take care of me. And he did."

For a moment, she was silent, and Katherine didn't know if she was through talking. The counselor in her waited for her to continue.

"First, he showed me his prostitution business. I remember thinking this was wrong, but what could I do? The man treated me like a princess and professed he loved me." She sighed. "I was so stupid. Even though I knew being a whore was demoralizing, I did nothing."

Shaking her head, she gazed at Katherine. "You probably think I'm a terrible person for not going to the police right then."

"No, I think you're trapped in a bad situation and don't know how to get out," she said, trying to soothe the young woman.

Katherine needed to gain her trust. To help the case, she wanted Isabella to tell her every horrifying juicy detail to help her break the bondage the pregnant woman found herself in.

"Against my parent's will, he convinced me to move in with him. Like a fool, I did, not realizing three other women lived with him. I was just the current flavor of the month. After all, I was supposed to be his queen."

What a shock to learn other women were in the same house with your boyfriend.

Rubbing her oversized belly, she stared off. "One day he came to me and said one of his girls couldn't work and someone had to fill in for her. Appalled he would want to share me, I immediately said no."

With a sigh, she shivered. "That's when he turned on the guilt. Mateo said I did not bring in any income into the home and all he needed was my help for one night. Finally, I gave in and that was my first night turning tricks."

Speechless, Katherine reached out and touched the young woman's arm, trying to comfort her. How quickly a situation could turn into something terrifying.

Isabella wiped away a tear. "For the last nine months, I keep asking myself how did I get here?"

The urge to go out and find Mateo overwhelmed Katherine with the need to fix his problem permanently. After she got through with him, he wouldn't be making babies anymore.

"After that I helped out on a regular basis. Until, I became pregnant. Every time, I tried to take birth control pills, he said no. They would make me fat. Well, look at me now."

Pushing her hair back, she twisted the blanket in her fingers. "Not knowing if this was Mateo's child or some other man's, I asked him to take a DNA test, and he said no, it didn't matter. Because the baby would be put up for adoption."

Inside Katherine imagined Isabella testifying against Mateo and how her words would reflect him as the monster he was.

With a sob, she placed her face in her hands and cried. "For weeks, I kept trying to talk him out of giving up our child, and he said, no. Then one day he brought in a new girl. No longer did he want me for his queen."

Shaking her head, she wiped tears from her face. "Two big burly guys took me out of the house and placed me in a car. That night, they transferred me to the house with this strange Hispanic couple who will not let me leave."

Clenching her fists, she shook her head clearly perplexed.

"Once the baby is born, the other girls in the house told me I'll be transported to a brothel in Mexico."

Damn, but Katherine had been right. The babies were being sold and then the women sent against their will to a hellhole where they would probably die. Being right discharged a tremor of disgust through her.

Crying, Isabella gazed at Katherine. "You're my hope. My only chance of escaping. Yet, I'm afraid. Where will I go? What about the baby?"

Standing, Katherine took her hand in hers, using all the counseling techniques she'd learned in the past few years.

"Detective Antonio and I found a safe place for you to stay until your delivery. At that time, you will make the decision whether to keep or give up your baby for adoption."

The girl's face brightened. "Once we resolve the case, I would recommend you contact your family. Work things out with them but wait until the investigation is over, because you don't want to put them in jeopardy."

Shaking her head vehemently, she said, "No, he would kill them just for revenge. Would you please make certain the police are watching out for them? Oh, no, I jeopardized their lives by leaving."

A suspicious look gathered in her eyes, and she bit her bottom lip. "When you say case, what do you mean?"

Now if she would answer her questions, this investigation would finally have its first break.

"The FBI and the Dallas Police Department are working together to rescue the girls and put Mateo behind bars. Do you mind answering a couple of questions?"

Isabella nodded her okay. "Do you know who was going to adopt the baby? Did you meet the people or have any contact with them?"

"No. It's all hidden, and Mateo said he will net about thirty-five thousand dollars after he pays the doctor, hospital, and lawyer. Staying at the house, I learned I'm not the only one. In fact, there are at least five women expecting."

That corresponded with the number the welfare worker told them about. But what would he do with these babies, especially if the mother refused to give them up for adoption?

"Do you know if the women who are pregnant are all treated the same way as you? Do they give up their babies?"

"No, some of them he took in and others were working girls that needed his help. Once they arrived, they were never allowed to leave. Someone watched us always. With cameras and a monitor."

Yet, they let her interview Isabella the first time.

"Why were you able to speak with me?"

A deep sigh released from the girl. "At first, they didn't want to, but they receive the money from the government, and they were afraid it would stop if they didn't let me talk to you. If I didn't answer correctly, they said they would kill me. And I feared them, but knew that if I did nothing, I would eventually die."

"Are there other girls there at the home?"

"Yes," she said softly.

Katherine wanted to run out the door and help these trapped

women escape. But she needed to wait on Detective Dickhead to go with her. They would rescue those women.

"So once your baby is born, Mateo has a family lined up to adopt the child. Then you would be sent across the border to Mexico against your will. To do what?"

"Work in a brothel in Mexico. Instead of believing his lies, how I wish I had gone to college."

Hopelessness filled her face. The way she seemed to sag against the bed. The woman had been through so much today. It was time to let her rest.

"Don't give up just yet. There may be a way out of this. Tonight I'm going to stay here with you, and in the morning, we'll escort you to a home until you have your child."

The girl nodded. "I'm going to close my eyes, I'm really tired."

Fewer than five minutes later, she was sound asleep. Sitting in a chair beside her, Katherine stared, wondering how the girl's life would have been different if she never met Mateo.

No matter how much she learned in counseling, there were just some people you wanted to slap up the side of the head and show them the damage they did to people.

Mateo needed a good castration. How she would love the opportunity to train being a surgeon on him, but her own counselor would tell her she was letting her emotions influence her decisions. And she would be right. Mateo was worse than a baby daddy.

Sometime around midnight, she dozed off and awoke as a struggling Isabella was being forced from the room. Pushing herself out of the chair, she hurried out the door, yanking out her taser.

"Let her go," she yelled.

Two men in masks continued hurrying her out the door of the hospital.

If she didn't stop them, the girl's life was over. Possibly even the baby's. Flinging herself onto one of their backs, she tased the man who roared in pain and dropped to the ground jerking, taking her with him. One down. The other man all but dragged Isabella across the parking lot. Soon, he would get away with her.

Pulling out her Glock, she screamed. "Stop or I'll shoot."

The man didn't heed her words and sitting on the concrete, she lifted her gun and fired at him.

With a scream, he went down, releasing Isabella, who hauled off and kicked him. "What part of no do you not understand."

At that moment, hospital security came running out the door. "Ma'am, are you all right."

The young man helped her to stand, and she pointed to the other jerk. "That one's been tased and the other one is shot."

A Dallas police squad car pulled into the lot, and she groaned. "Detective Dickhead."

"What?" the security guard asked.

She ignored him as the handsome man ran up beside her. "Are you okay?"

What did he think that because she knocked the guy to the ground, she was all beat up? A little sore, but she would suck it up and bear the pain. After everything Isabella had been through, that was the least she could endure.

"Never been better," she said. "That goon there needs to be interrogated. The second one, he's not going to be available for some time. He took a bullet to the thigh, so he's probably not going to be able to dance for a while."

"Go home and rest. I'll take over for the rest of the night."

Actually, that sounded wonderful. Isabella's story upset her, and she tried very hard to hide her wound behind being tough, but this one would haunt her. A young woman trusting a man who promised her everything she wanted and then sold her into prostitution. The ugliness overwhelmed Katherine.

Turning, she grabbed Antonio's shirt and hauled him in close. His masculine scent filled her lungs, leaving her dizzy, and she had the most incredible urge to kiss him, but that would be crazy.

"Leave the girl alone. Tonight, she gave me some answers we need," she said her voice rough with the emotion she tried to hide.

"From the looks of it, she's going to be busy. Her water just broke."

CHAPTER 11

*A*fter only a few hours of sleep, Katherine had gone into the Lipstick and Lead Agency, determined to write up a report of everything the girl told her last night before she forgot.

It was after nine o'clock when she arrived. The place was silent, like no one was there, and she knew that couldn't be true. She checked Jennifer's office, empty. Brittany's empty. Even Shaggy and Jon Paul's offices were empty.

As she strolled through the main area a strange noise came from her uncle's office. "Oh, oh, oh, Big Daddy, you know how to ride a big girl like me."

What the hell? She walked closer and the sounds coming from inside made her stomach revolt. Hitting the record button on her phone, she recorded the noises, because she wanted someone else to verify what she was hearing.

"Oh, Big Daddy, do it again," she screamed.

That was all she could take. Hitting stop on her phone, she turned and walked into her office and slammed the door, letting them know someone had arrived. If they wanted to do the nasty, they needed to find a location other than the agency where they worked.

In about ten minutes, she heard Gina giggling outside as she hurried to the ladies' room. Just gross. Now it would be hard to go in there without thinking about the two of them...

Jennifer came walking in. "Good morning, Gina."

"Morning, sunshine, how are you feeling today."

"Like hell," she said and strolled into Katherine's office. "How's the investigation going."

"Oh my. Why are you late?"

Her cousin shrugged her shoulders. "Slept in with my husband this morning. Is that a crime? Will I be fired or sent to jail?"

"Jail time. Because when I came in here, no one was here but Uncle Sam and Gina and they were locked up in his office shagging each other."

Shock and disgust rolled over Jennifer's face. "No. Please tell me no."

"Listen to this," she said and hit the play button.

As the recording played, Katherine watched her cousin lean over the trash can and retch. Though it didn't last long, she had a clear sense about what was happening behind that closed door. How could she ever go into her Uncle Sam's office without picturing Gina spread across his desk. Gross.

"Stop, you're making me ill," Jennifer cried.

Brittany walked into Katherine's office and stared at the two of them. "Oh no, this doesn't look good. What's going on?"

"Listen," Katherine said and hit the play on her phone.

"Nooooo," Brittany said. "Is that Uncle Sam and Gina? Where did you get that?"

Funny how they all couldn't believe their uncle and Gina were happy. The two people had walked around with the biggest grins. Their hands lingering.

"This morning," Jennifer said. "Everyone was late and when Katherine arrived, they were locked up in Uncle Sam's office, and she was feeding him his biscuits and gravy."

"Ohhhh," Katherine said. "Did you have to ruin the food for me? Now I will never eat that again."

Brittany giggled. "We should have seen this coming. Uncle Sam has not been able to keep from dipping his wick in any available--"

"Don't say it. And Gina always advertised she was available. But I never thought they would actually act upon their urges," Katherine said.

While the two lovebirds created quite a stir, Katherine needed to hurry.

"What are you going to do with that recording?" Jennifer asked.

"Hang on to it for now. What are we going to do about this little affair? Office romances bring all kinds of legal problems."

The three women sighed. "Didn't need this first thing," Jennifer said. "I'm tired. I'm emotional, and dang but my breasts feel like they've been squeezed into a vise, and they're hard as rocks."

Katherine and Brittany glanced at each other. "Did you ever take a pregnancy test?"

"I'm not pregnant."

"All right," Brittany said, "but you sure act like a pregnant woman."

"I'm not pregnant," Jennifer said, rising.

"Again, what are we going to do about this situation?" Katherine asked, trying to bring their focus back to the problem at hand. What to do about Gina donging their uncle. Not the fact Jennifer had the symptoms of an expecting woman.

A frown crossed Jennifer's face. "At this moment, I can't make any rational decisions. Let's wait and see how this plays out. How is your investigation going?"

"The man is dealing not only in sex trafficking, but black-market babies. He's a real piece of shit."

The three women groaned.

"And how is working with Detective Baby Daddy?"

What could she say, so far they tolerated each other, though every time she glanced at him, her pulse sped up a little faster. But there wasn't a man alive that she couldn't resist, and he would be easy after how he treated his daughter.

"Peachy," she said. "Just peachy. Now get out of my office, I've got notes to write and then I have to return to the hospital. We're having a baby."

The two women stopped and stared at her. Katherine laughed. "One of the girls we picked up yesterday went into labor."

Rolling their eyes, they walked out the door.

"Damn, must be something in the water," Katherine said to the empty office.

CHAPTER 12

*A*round ten o'clock, Katherine walked in the door. "What did she have?"

He shook his head. Babies arrived in their own sweet time and this one must know his life was going to be difficult, so he was taking his time.

"Nothing yet. First babies can take a while."

Why was he talking about a subject he never had experienced? Why was he acting like just because he had a ten-year-old daughter, he was the guru on parenting. Sometimes it felt like Emma was the one teaching him, not the other way around.

"We need to talk," he said, thinking now would be a good time to clear the air about their differences. Their investigation had only just begun, and he would rather be working with his partner than just tolerating each other. Especially in a life or death situation.

"Yes, we do," she said, her voice growing excited. "Last night, Isabella and I had a nice long conversation, and she gave me all the dirt she had on Mateo."

Why did she believe she told her everything? This man's lists of crimes seemed to be expanding and the sooner they had him behind bars, the easier Antonio would breathe. Whenever he was dealing with a real scumbag, he worried about them hurting his family, his daughter.

For the next few minutes, she rambled about what the girl said, his anger increasing by the minute at the way Mateo treated her. The thought of someone doing this to his baby girl would send him straight into orbit. He'd find himself behind bars. Not good.

"Sorry they almost got away with getting her back. Did you learn anything from interrogating those two pieces of shit?"

Those men clammed up tighter than a virgin at an orgy.

"They're not talking yet. Once the district attorney lays the charges on them, they might change their minds."

They could tell them who hired them and where they were taking Isabella. Whatever information they had would help their investigation. After the last twenty-four hours, he was determined Mateo would find himself living the life of luxury down at the county jail.

"Doubtful, because if they are connected with Mateo, then they will be serving some serious time. All they got here is a misdemeanor."

"Oh no, I'm trying to charge them with attempted kidnapping of a witness. If we can get her to turn state witness, then as soon as we catch Mateo, his operation will be swarmed by the Feds."

Katherine nodded. "Do you think they have knowledge about his black-market adoption service?"

"Great question," he said, knowing he needed to bring up what was bothering him, but they were making this partnership work. When he mentioned his discomfort, he already knew her reaction.

Explosion. Fireworks and water cannons all at once. But he had to try.

"There's something else we need to discuss. If we're going to be working together, we must get along and watch each other's backs."

Would she react kindly with his request for her not to shoot from the hip? Not to totally hate him?

Her eyebrows rose, and he could see her mind twirling with the possibilities of what he was about to say. She leaned against the wall and crossed her arms, her dark eyes sparkled with something that looked like bemusement. He wasn't certain, and he wasn't going to take any chances.

"Katherine, I don't understand why you dislike me so much."

She shrugged. "I don't dislike you. I almost hate you."

"Why what did I do to you?"

"I know your secrets," she said, "And that's all I'm prepared to say. But you're right about saying we need to work together. I'll always be cordial to you. I'll protect and serve and cover your back. That doesn't mean I have to like you."

How could you claim to dislike someone and not explain the reasons why? What kind of unfair deal was this?

"What the hell secrets are you talking about?" he asked. "I don't have any secrets."

"Detective Baby Daddy, I promise to protect and serve your sorry ass during this investigation, but once it's over, we go back to total disliking one another."

Frustrated out of his mind, he grabbed her by the arm and stopped her from walking out the door. "See, that is what I'm asking about. Why do you insist on calling me that jackass name? I'm not a baby daddy."

"Yeah, and I'm not a McKenzie," she said. Leaning into him, she took a deep breath. "You always smell so manly."

With a gentle shove, he pushed her away. "Let's roll. We need to go to the house and see if there are any other girls there. Last night, I was issued a search warrant."

As they walked out of the office, he wanted to growl with frustration. The woman irritated him beyond measure and he still didn't understand why she refused to tell him why she called him that despicable name.

CHAPTER 13

Inside, Katherine was laughing. She was getting to the man. Calling him Detective Baby Daddy seemed to frustrate the hell out of him and that made her happy.

No, she couldn't talk about how she knew of his past, but she knew the truth. She'd heard it from his own daughter. The man may have cleaned up his act in recent years, but he'd been a typical baby daddy, running off and leaving his pregnant girlfriend.

Those types of men needed castration or sterilization or something to keep them from fathering children they didn't want to raise. Just thinking about the way her own father had done her and how Emma's father hurt her, left her shaking with anger.

If she didn't think he was so darn handsome, she would be tempted to look the other direction when the bullets started flying. But then again, that would be murder, and she had no desire to go to jail. And his daughter didn't deserve that kind of treatment.

"Doesn't look like anyone's home," she said as they pulled up in front of the house.

The house appeared almost deserted and that sent a chill

racing down her spine. Had they removed the girls and where would they take them?

"Take the lead," he said as they got out of the car.

Surprised, she turned and stared at him. "Why? You always want to have the lead."

"Maybe I'm trying to be nice," he said.

"Maybe you're hoping I'll be the first one shot," she said.

"Maybe you're right."

She grinned at him. "Don't count on it. I'm going to sidestep and you'll be right behind me."

"Just shut up and do your job," he said.

"Gladly," she said and pounded on the door. "Police, search warrant."

"You aren't the police," he said.

"Well, I didn't hear your happy-go-lucky voice shouting out instructions."

Silence. There was nothing.

Grabbing the front door handle, she tried the door and it was locked.

"What now, genius?" she asked as she walked over to the garage window and peered inside. Nothing. Empty.

"Let's walk around the back." Together, they eased toward the rear of the house. As they crept through the yard toward the windows, a tiny voice called out, "Whatcha doin'?"

With a jerk she, glanced up to see a small child about seven staring over the top of the wooden fence.

"Shh, we're chasing bad guys."

"Nobody's home," he said.

They both froze and stared at the boy. Katherine asked, "How do you know?"

"A truck came and took away their stuff."

"Did you see any pregnant girls?" Antonio asked.

The kid giggled. "My daddy told my mommy not to drink their water. There were five ladies with big tummies."

"Did they leave with the truck?"

The little boy shrugged and someone called his name. "Gotta go, my mommy's calling."

With a sigh, they turned and gazed at each other. "We're a little late."

Antonio peered in the back windows of the house and turned back to her. "Empty. They're gone."

"What about mail?"

Surely, they left a forwarding address and hurried back to the front of the house.

When they came around the corner, a lady was searching through the mailbox.

"Stop, police," Antonio called.

Her eyes widened, and she ran back to her car, jumped in and took off.

They hurried to their ugly car and Antonio started off after her. As he gunned the rattle trap vehicle, Katherine buckled her seat belt.

"Come one," she said. "She's getting away. Can't this piece of junk go any faster."

Not answering, Antonio focused on driving. The lady turned down a street and he laughed. "We got her."

"What?"

"Dead end."

When she realized she was in a no outlet, she whirled the car around, but Antonio had blocked her in the road. She jumped out of the old Buick and started to run.

"Get the pregnant girl," he said.

With a smirk, Katherine watched as he tackled the older woman to the ground, slipping plastic ties around her wrist and reciting her Maranda rights.

Katherine walked up to the window of her car and peered in. "Hi," she said.

A young blonde girl with big blue eyes sat there trembling.

"Are you all right?"

"Why are they hurting, Ms. Smith?"

"Nah, she's being cuffed because she refused to stop, and she ran. What's your name?"

Tears welled up in her eyes, and she was shaking uncontrollably.

"Olivia Jones," she said.

"How old are you?"

"Eighteen," she replied. "I'd really like to go home."

"Where is home?"

"Minneapolis, Minnesota," she said. "Please call my mother. I want to go home."

Sadness overwhelmed Katherine and once again, she wanted to castrate Mateo. "Honey, you come down to the precinct and tell your story to Detective Antonio and me and I promise you, I'll call your mother."

The girl sniffed and wiped away the tears from her eyes. "He won't be there will he?"

"Who?"

"Mateo?"

"No, we haven't caught him yet. But we're working on capturing him. And we'll keep you safe. Do you want Ms. Smith to know you're talking to the police?"

"No," Olivia said her eyes wide. "She works for him. They'll kill me." She clutched her Katherine's arm. "Act like I'm resisting. Don't let her think I'm saying anything to you."

Katherine liked this play acting. With a smile at Olivia, she screamed. "It would be better for you, if you cooperated. We're hauling you off to jail."

The detective turned and stared at her like she was crazy. That just made the experience of rescuing this girl even more enjoyable.

"How far along are you?" Katherine asked, fearing they would cause her to go into labor.

"Only seven months," she said. "I want to go home."

"Give me a minute or two, and we'll get you out of here," she promised the young woman.

"This way, Miss Jones, if you don't cooperate, we have a cell waiting for you."

After backup arrived, the detective shoved Ms. Smith into a patrol car, the woman resisting him every step of the way. Finally, he buckled her in, closed the door and spoke to the patrolman.

He walked over to her side and gazed at her like she was completely out of her mind.

"What are you doing?"

"We've got to keep them separated," Katherine told Antonio. "This is Olivia Jones from Minnesota. She's a missing girl, and she wants to answer questions, but not let her captors realize she's talking to us."

Antonio picked up his phone and made a call.

"Agent White, I'm sending to the downtown station a Ms. Smith, caretaker for the girls. Meet her at headquarters. I'm taking another girl to a different precinct. Yes, sir, I understand, but the girl is going to talk only if Ms. Smith doesn't know or Mateo."

Standing in the street, talking to the FBI agent, Antonio appeared irritated.

Working with the agency had so far been a challenge, trying to meet their expectations.

"Of course," he said and hung up the phone. "Jerk. After we talk to her, he will come interview Olivia. He'll come to where we are. Is she all right?"

"Terrified and she wants her mother."

"Let's go take her statement."

CHAPTER 14

*A*ntonio watched Katherine bring the young girl a bottle of water. "You doing all right?" she asked her.

"Yes." She sat the box of Kleenex next to her.

Her story sounded so much like Isabella's and yet more twisted because she had only been seventeen when she'd been taken from right outside her high school.

Another underage girl, another crime committed by Mateo.

"I've called your parents," Katherine said. "Your mother started crying when I told her we found you. Once we have you settled in a secure location, you can call them. Your mother is going to fly out in the morning to come pick you up."

The family must be feeling joy that she had been located. Antonio couldn't imagine the fear, the excitement, and relief knowing their child had been rescued.

The young woman began to cry again. "I thought I was going to die."

Katherine took her hand in hers. "Look, you have gone through so much. Even though you're going home, life is going to be difficult for a while. It will be an adjustment for you, your parents and the people who care about you. Never feel like this is your fault. Find a good counselor and get into therapy. Don't let this one incident in your life control you. You're a survivor."

"Did you tell my mother I'm pregnant?"

"No, honey, I thought you should tell her."

With a sigh, Antonio kept imagining she was his daughter. How would he react?

"Thank you," she said.

The girl took a deep breath. "They already had a couple for the baby. Part of me thinks I should give him up for adoption, but then I think this is my child too."

As a father, there were so many things Antonio wanted to say to her, but this was not his business. The girl's family should be the one to counsel her on what was best for her and the baby.

He liked the fact that Katherine told her to do counseling, and actually, that kind of surprised him. She handled the suggestion very well, and he wondered if she had any training in the area.

Agent White walked into the room.

"Olivia, this is Agent White from the FBI. He's here to ask you some questions. If you become tired, let us know."

"Can I have a hamburger? I'm starving. We could only eat the meals they prepared for us."

Katherine stood. "I'll order one now."

As she stepped out of the room, Antonio was amazed at the way she seemed to genuinely care about the wellbeing of the girls they rescued. In some ways, she related to them better than either him or the FBI suit.

"Olivia, let me begin by saying I'm so sorry you were abducted. We're doing everything we can to capture the men responsible for this. Can you tell me how old you were when they took you?" the agent asked.

The young woman took a deep breath and released it, a shiver rippling through her body as she began to tell the tale.

"It was the last week of my senior year in school. At the time, I was seventeen. That day, I stayed late working on a project with some other students. When I left the building, the sun was setting and as I walked down the street, a van pulled up and two men jumped out and grabbed me."

Antonio's insides squeezed tightly and his chest pounded. What if this happened to his daughter? An innocent young girl just walking home. No matter what, he needed to protect Emma.

There would come a day when Emma would want to do something he considered dangerous, and they would argue over this imaginary drama. An innocent like Emma wouldn't see the meanness in the world like he did.

For the next thirty minutes, she spoke to the agent, confirming what she told him and Katherine earlier.

"After a girl had her baby she disappeared from the house. At first, I feared we were no longer useful to them, and they would kill us. One girl in the house was having her second child. Once we recovered from childbirth, she said we would be transported to Mexico to turn tricks in the brothels there."

The girl hung her head and sobbed. "How do I tell my parents?"

Walking over to Olivia, Katherine took her hand. "They love you. Your mother was so excited you had been found. You'll work this out. With the help of therapy, you'll get through this."

The young woman took a deep breath and gained control of her tears.

"Can you tell us the location of where you worked here in the states?"

Thank goodness, he didn't use the words hooker or whore, because this child was innocent of any wrongdoing.

"Here in Dallas. We did not walk the streets, but they kept us in an industrial building they converted into where we lived and worked."

"But you don't know where?"

"Close to downtown. Because I could look out the window

and see the building with the red horse on the side not far from us."

"That's on Commerce Street in downtown," the agent said. "And men came to the location?"

"Yes, sir," she said. "Some were regulars."

The FBI suit asked her a thousand more questions and each one left Antonio more and more disgusted with the human race. If ever he felt the need to go home, take a shower and hug his daughter, it was today.

The afternoon sun had long ago descended into the western sky and the urge to protect Olivia was strong. No one was going to take this girl like they did Isabella. Not unless they wanted a bullet.

Knowing a long night lay ahead of him, he called Mrs. Langford, a widow who stayed with Emma and told her he would not be home tonight. In his home, the woman had her own bedroom and was used to being asked to come stay with Emma. She was a lifeline he needed on investigations like this.

Now nearly midnight, exhaustion filled the young woman's face.

"Time to end this," Katherine said. "She's stressed and she needs to rest."

The agent sighed and stood. "I think we've got everything we need."

"Tonight, you're going to stay at a local hotel here. One of us will be in the room next to you," Katherine told her.

No, after the last incident at the hospital, they would both be staying with her, with connecting rooms on the fifteenth floor. Antonio had gone to extreme measures to make certain there wasn't a repeat of what happened with Isabella.

The only problem...spending the night with Katherine in a hotel room.

CHAPTER 15

Well, crap! Antonio insisted they spend the night in the hotel with Olivia after what happened at the hospital. Now here they were in a downtown hotel, on the fifteenth floor with adjoining rooms.

Sleeping in the same room, with their clothes on, even with the door open between them, felt way more intimate than she expected. The hotel provided them each with a toothbrush and Olivia slept in the room next to them.

Before they left the station, she'd been given the opportunity to call her mother and the crying at their reunion ripped Katherine's heart out of her chest. Her own mother and she had a tenuous relationship, but still when something bad happened, she was the first person Katherine wanted.

Just like Olivia.

Exhausted, the girl went into her room and crawled into bed. Katherine checked her door to make certain the inside remained locked, latched, and no one could get in. Leaving the door between their rooms open, she prayed for a quiet night where everyone rested.

With the lights turned off, Detective Dickhead lay in his bed, and she in hers. A nightstand between the two beds. Still, the fact he was a foot from her made her uneasy.

The entire day had been unnerving. Capturing Olivia and her keeper, then listening to how she was kidnapped, the sounds of her weeping echoed in her brain.

"Are you asleep?" he asked.

"No," she said quietly. How could she sleep with the thought of what happened to Olivia pressuring her to find the others?

"Tough day."

"One of the worst," she replied.

She rolled to her side and faced him, and he did the same.

"She's a strong young woman."

"Still, how can people hurt each other this way," she said, trying to rationalize what Mateo had done to who knows how many girls. While she knew being a counselor would have its bad days, so did being a bounty hunter.

"I don't understand. Unless they've been damaged so badly that they no longer care."

"Still an innocent kid abducted walking home," she said. "Any one of us are susceptible to a kidnapping crime."

"It makes me want to lock my daughter up, and yet, she would hate me."

Everything she learned about Emma came rushing back though his voice sounded like he cared for her. Like she meant everything to him and that didn't make sense to her.

"Young women don't realize the danger out in the world and their naivety makes them vulnerable."

"Yes," he said. "Kids don't believe bad things will happen to them. And it can occur to anyone."

Except the kids in her group understood from personal experience bad things happened. Those children grew up watching their parents fight and argue, breakup and makeup, and start all over again with someone new. Those children lived with the awareness that life was not always happy.

Part of her wanted to tell him his daughter was a resilient young girl who knew better than to think everything was roses. Her father left her when she was young, and her mother had been shot and killed in the line of duty. Oh, yes, Emma was well aware life could be harsh and brutal at times.

They needed to quit talking about Emma, or she would explode. What made him change from the arrogant young man who didn't need a family to the man he was today? The police force? Or losing his wife?

"People don't believe terrible things will happen to them," she said, thinking of clients who broke their bail agreements and were shocked when they went back to jail.

"Do you ever want to move to a deserted island away from people?" he asked.

For a moment, she thought about his question. "When I was younger and didn't understand why things happened to me, yes. But I love my work, my cousins, and what we're doing with the business. Plus, I'll soon have my masters..."

"What? How come I don't know this? What are you getting your masters in?"

A trickle of unease spiraled through Katherine. Talking about her college education was dangerous as she didn't want him to become too curious and learn his daughter belonged to her therapy group. Because then he would know why she hated him.

Though she had to admit working with him, she was seeing a different side of the man. A side that was warm and friendly and a confident officer of the law.

But all the years of hard work and going to school, she would not hide. Even from Detective Dickhead.

"Counseling."

"Oh, that explains why you handled Olivia so well today. I was really proud of the way you encouraged her to get help."

"Thank you," she said a warmth spreading through her. For a second, she appreciated that they were talking to each other in the dark in a personal way that left them both vulnerable.

"After my wife was killed, I put Emma in counseling. To help her deal with the changes in her life. My daughter comes home and tells me we're so blessed. I'm just grateful the sessions are helping her."

How did she respond to that? When she knew Emma struggled with what he had done to her? How he abandoned them when she was a baby? There were two sides to every story, and she had been advised to always consider everyone's side. Was she missing something here? Could Emma have not been truthful?

At the moment, her brain was exhausted, and sleep refused to come.

"How are you doing since your wife died?"

The question came out of nowhere, and yet she needed the answer.

Silence filled the night and finally in a cracked voice he said, "Three years have passed and the time seems like yesterday. Like we said earlier, you never think something bad is going to happen to you. Yet Sheila prepared for her dying just in case. She was the planner, not me. More than anything I miss my companion, my lover, my best friend."

Stunned, Katherine lay there, sorrow filling her at his heartache.

"Sometimes life sucks," she said.

He gave a chuckle. "Yeah, it does."

Sadness filled Katherine, though her life was very busy, she never experienced that kind of love. Had never thought of wanting or needing a companion so much that when they were gone, it left a hole in your heart. Certainly, her parents never experienced love that bound them together for better or worse.

In the darkness, Katherine realized tonight bonded them in ways she never expected. Though she still didn't like how he treated Emma when she was a small child, the man also loved his daughter and had fiercely loved his wife. Maybe there was more to him than she dreamed possible.

His soft steady breathing let her know he had fallen asleep. Tonight she would watch over them and keep them safe.

CHAPTER 16

The next afternoon, Antonio stood outside when the bell rang and hundreds of children came spilling out the doors of the school. Waiting for his daughter at their meeting place, he gazed at all the young girls. Little did they know the danger the world presented them.

When Emma came out the door, she waved goodbye to her friend and came running toward him. The sight of her happy face filled him with so much joy. His chest ached with happiness as he hugged her to him.

Her small frame had yet to develop into womanhood, and he was grateful. Though her cherub face, blonde hair and blue eyes held promises of beauty in the years to come.

"Dad, you're going to embarrass me."

"Sorry, but I needed some love after a terrible day and night."

Though the night had been strange. Listening to Olivia terrified him, but lying in the darkness and talking with Katherine had been different. In many ways, he now felt closer to her than anyone.

They talked about things that troubled him, and then he fell asleep. Thank goodness, the long night was uneventful and when he awoke this morning, Katherine lay sleeping curled on her side.

Her dark hair had been brushed back. In sleep, her features were more beautiful because they were relaxed, and she didn't look like she was ready to kick the world in the ass.

When she woke, they ordered room service and made certain Olivia had plenty to eat. Katherine tried to keep the talk upbeat and not on the events of the day before.

About noon, Olivia's mother arrived, and the reunion had them all crying. While she told her mother of her pregnancy, when her mother saw her she sobbed overjoyed her daughter was alive. A joyous reuniting he would never forget.

Tonight, Olivia and her mother were staying at the hotel and Katherine would be in the same room next door, but he made the decision to go home to Emma.

"Were you on a bad case?" she asked as they walked toward the car.

While they seldom talked of his job, she would often recognize when an investigation bothered him. "Yes, one that made me want to come home and protect my girl."

"Oh, Daddy, I'm safe. Mrs. Langford is the one who needs protecting," she said with a laugh. "Poor dear fell asleep in the chair and I had to wake her up and send her to bed."

The day was coming when he would have to find someone Emma couldn't manipulate. But hopefully that was years down the road.

As they reached the vehicle, he turned and gazed at her.

"Honey, there is something we've never talked about. Because I'm a detective, I work on cases that cause me as a father to always be aware of how vulnerable young girls are. Please promise me you will never ever leave a party or school after dark. No matter where you are, I will come get you and take you home. If I can't, I will have someone pick you up."

How he wished he could tell her the dangers she could face,

but he didn't want to completely tarnish her innocence that he found so endearing.

She laughed. "Daddy, they taught me stranger danger in kindergarten. No, I'm not getting into a car with anyone I don't know."

That was a relief, but still Olivia wasn't given an option.

"Thank you, but sometimes they don't give you a choice. That's why I don't want you walking anywhere after dark, even with your friends. Call me, I'll come get you."

After hearing Olivia's tale of how they took her, he wanted to make certain she understood the rules.

"All right, but there is a party I'm wanting to go to in two weeks," she said.

Something about the way she said the words, made him uneasy. "Do I know the parents?"

"I'm not sure. A girl in my group. She's having a party for everyone"

"I'll have to meet her parents and see if I like them or not."

With a heavy sigh, she shook her head. "Sometimes it's not easy having parents--" She stopped, and he realized she was thinking about her mother. He watched as she closed her eyes, and then she took a deep breath to release the hurt. "A father who works on the police force."

Was this group helping her? Before, she would have broken down and cried, but now she took several calming breaths and released the pain, which is what the counselor told her to do. Even after three years, they both occasionally stumbled over the words that once included his wife.

"No, it's not," he said. "Come on, let's get home. I'm hoping Mrs. Langford brought over some delicious homemade pot roast."

He backed the car out and started toward home. The word sending warmth through him.

"She did," Emma said. "Oh, and Daddy, I need you to sign some papers for school."

This is what he missed last night. A typical night of them discussing her schoolday, doing her homework, and family time at the dinner table. Only now, instead of three, there was only the two of them.

CHAPTER 17

Katherine walked into her apartment and knew it had been a mistake to give her mother a key.

"Dear, you're finally home," she said, coming out of the kitchen. "I was starting to get worried."

"Hi, Mom, what are you doing here?" she asked, thinking how tonight she had been looking forward to alone time. After the last few days, she needed some time to recover and rejuvenate. Some time to mediate and go back and read some of the files on the girls in her therapy group.

"Sorry, for two days, I spent working an investigation that kept me very busy," she said.

Her sister Nicole and nephew Grayson came from the guest bedroom. Which meant they probably were spending the night.

"Hey, we've been worried about you. Mom tried to call."

"Yesterday, I turned my phone off while I worked a case," she said. "Even now, I haven't looked at my messages. What's the occasion?"

"You don't remember?" Nicole said her eyes growing large as she held onto Grayson who was chewing on a toy. "Mom's birthday."

Oh, shit. The last few days had been so gut wrenching, she completely forgot all about her mother's birthday. "I'm sorry, Mom. This is your day and I forgot."

"It's all right. It's only my seventieth. Nothing big or important," she said, draining the spaghetti noodles.

One thing her mother could do well was lay on the holy guilt when Katherine's life was crazy. When all she wanted to do was crawl in bed and read a little before going to sleep.

When she still needed to think about her reaction to Detective Dickhead last night. Lying in the dark seemed so intimate talking about the things that bothered them about their jobs. Learning he really loved his wife and even to this day, had feelings for her. Most shocking was how he never wanted another relationship.

"You're having to cook your own birthday celebration dinner. When this case is over, I'll take you out."

"You're on a case?" Nicole asked, rocking the baby in her arms.

"The worst investigation I've ever dealt with," she said as she headed toward her bedroom knowing she had to change out of the same clothes she'd been wearing for two days. Maybe new clothes would revive her, and she could at least celebrate with them.

The sight of her own bed was enough to make her want to lie down. But she feared she would never get up and this was an important day in the life of her mother.

Quickly, she put on a comfortable dress she wore around the house. When she came out of the bedroom, her mother was pouring the wine and setting the table.

Nicole stood around holding her son. As much as Katherine loved him, she thought of Isabella and Olivia and witnessed her sister's life in theirs. Only Nicole had bad taste in men.

She lifted Grayson from Nicole's arms. "Hey, baby, how are you? Have you missed your aunt Katherine?"

The baby squealed with delight and kicked his feet and legs in happiness. "You're so cute."

"Look, two teeth," Nicole said.

Like a dutiful aunt, Katherine gazed inside her nephew's mouth to see his first teeth.

Knowing she should help her mother, but her reserves were completely drained, Katherine held onto to her nephew tightly. After everything, she experienced in the last two days, this child was so blessed.

"Your sister has news," her mother said.

What now? Another baby? No matter how they tried to warn her about David, Nicole had been madly in love and soon pregnant. And where was David? He disappeared into the woods and when he came out, Katherine stood waiting for him with a warrant.

Father of a child, you pay your child support or you give up all your rights. For all women, she threw in a stipulation he must receive a vasectomy so no other girl would have to raise a baby of his without any financial help.

The man gave penniless a whole new meaning. His belongings consisted of a van—his love nest that needed a new paint job. While he balked at the clipping, with no lawyer, he soon came back to her with a document from the doctor showing he'd been snipped.

With no regrets, her sister signed the paperwork he would not be liable for child support, but he had no rights to his son.

One less baby daddy maker in the world.

"We're waiting," Katherine finally said, knowing she must sound like a cranky old woman. "Please don't tell me you're expecting again."

A curse escaped Nicole. "Why is it you ruin everything?"

That was fair. "You're right, I'm sorry, I should not have said that," Katherine replied thinking she was wrong. Only the last time she said *I have news*, she was pregnant. "What is your news?"

Her sister sighed and held up a letter. "I've been accepted into the University of North Texas nursing program."

This was great. Not that Grayson wasn't fabulous. "Congratulations. That's wonderful."

"Both of my girls are going to be college graduates. I'm so proud of you," her mother said, coming out of the kitchen and giving them a hug along with Grayson.

"Sis, I have a favor to ask," Nicole said.

"This I don't agree with," her mother said, huffing back to the stove.

"While I'm going to school, I'd like to work part-time at Lipstick and Lead. No, I don't know much about bounty hunting, but I need a part-time job I can work and also take the baby."

Pans could be heard slamming in Katherine's kitchen. When her mother became angry, everyone knew of her unhappiness. And unfortunately, Katherine often recognized herself in her mother.

"Let me talk to Jennifer and Brittany. But you don't want Gina taking care of the baby, so it might be time to consider either a babysitter or nursery."

"I promise to work hard, so I can pay for school and earn my degree."

"Come on, girls, let's eat. This is my birthday celebration and as busy as you two are, who knows when we'll all be together again."

Inside, Katherine cringed. Why did her mother need to make her feel like she was never a good enough daughter? Even if she moved back home and saw her every minute, it would not be enough.

Nicole coming to work for the agency could be a perfect solution. Especially if Jennifer was pregnant.

CHAPTER 18

The next morning, Chad met Antonio and Katherine at the precinct at eight o'clock.

"Good morning," he said, walking into the conference room.

Antonio's boss, Kevin was there, which made him nervous. Something was up and that left him anxious. The bosses had either cooked up a scheme or decided to remove them from the case.

When she walked in the door, Katherine gave him a nonchalant nod. While they no longer seemed to be going for each other's throats, things now seemed awkward between them.

Spending the night in a hotel room together brought them closer. But now he was very aware of how attractive she looked. The way, she smelled and the way her hair was fixed. Everything about her, he was ultra-sensitive to.

"Good job on rescuing the two girls, but we all know there are more, and Olivia mentioned the whore house is somewhere in downtown close to the Pegasus."

Chad took a sip of his coffee. "One of my colleagues pointed out a club is in that area. A known hangout for men and women to pick up someone."

"We're looking for a whorehouse, not a Tender dating location," Katherine said.

Thankfully, Antonio had not been drinking coffee, or he would have spewed the liquid causing a scene.

"Yes, but several women disappeared out of this club and have never been seen again," he said. "One girl woke up in a broken-down car. We think she barely escaped being taken."

Oh, yes, they were cooking up a scheme of some kind and a bad feeling came over Antonio.

"What's the name of this place?"

"Saul's," Chad said. "We want Katherine to go in and seek out Mateo. If this is one of his places for him to find John's, then he could possibly be working the joint."

A chill spiraled down Antonio's spine. Katherine was a woman not to be reckoned with, but Mateo had no heart or soul. Suddenly Antonio feared what the scumbag would do to hurt this woman that intrigued him. No, there could never be anything between them, but he didn't want her placed in danger.

"When?" she asked.

"Tonight," he said. "We're still trying to convince the older woman to talk, but she's not saying much right now. Surely, she knows where the other girls were taken, so I'm working on ways to take her confession."

The old lady must realize the amount of trouble they were all in once they locate Mateo.

"The two of you are going out clubbing tonight and if Mateo is out partying, you're going to be successful in bringing him in. Katherine, I would like for you to wear a wire. That way if something goes wrong, we can rush in and rescue you."

She nodded, her mouth tight. The urge to kiss her and tell her it was going to be all right almost overwhelmed him.

"So, we're searching for two places. One is the house where they've taken the pregnant women and the other is a whorehouse in downtown Dallas."

"Yes," Chad said. "No need for me to remind each of you how dangerous this situation is. Eyes and ears will be on Katherine tonight when she goes inside. Katherine, if something doesn't seem right, you have the right to end the operation."

That made Antonio feel a little better, but not much. Once they located the whorehouse, he felt certain they would catch Mateo, but first, they needed to locate the gentlemen's club.

"Do we understand each other?"

"And you won't be going with us?"

"No, I'm going to be working on Ruth Ortez, the caretaker. After we took her fingerprints, we learned her name. But an associate of mine will be with you."

Great, the big FBI man would not be there. Why wouldn't he wait and interrogate her more tomorrow? Sometimes Antonio didn't understand how the different law agencies worked.

"Once you capture Mateo, I expect to be notified right away."

Of course, he did, so he could take credit for the operation that captured the sex trafficker.

After everyone filed out, it was just him and Katherine. He gazed at her and she frowned.

"That FBI dude, he likes to give orders," she said. "The man does realize I'm not a cop, right?"

Antonio laughed. "If you don't want to do this, don't."

Though, he knew if she refused, she would be kicked off the case, and he didn't want that. So far, they had rescued two girls, but now he wanted to rescue them all, and he wanted Katherine working by his side.

A frown crossed her face. "Who said I didn't want to do it? I just don't like the way he tells us how to do our job. Even though I'm not getting paid for this. I'm just trying to save our bail money. Our agency better get some acknowledgment for bringing in a bail jumper when we capture the jerk."

"FBI boy will take all the glory," he said.

"Believe me, if I didn't know what these girls went through, I might back out, but after talking to Olivia and Isabella, I want him captured. I want his balls squeezed so tightly, they pop out his eyeballs. I want him to see his stable of hookers and pregnant women all set free while he sits behind bars."

Their feelings regarding Mateo were mutual.

"You wearing that hot pink dress again tonight?"

"Yeah, what's it to you?"

"Because I like how you look in pink," he said, thinking it was going to be hard to keep his hands off her.

"Well, Detective Baby Daddy, look all you want, but don't even think about touching the goods," she said as she stood and walked out the door.

Damn, once again, he was back to Detective Baby Daddy. Why did she persist on calling him that ugly name? He had no secrets to hide. Everyone knew everything about him, especially after Sheila died. For weeks, the papers ran articles on their life together and the daughter they shared.

But was Detective Baby Daddy any better than Detective Dickhead? And tonight, they were going clubbing.

CHAPTER 19

Once again, Katherine found herself in a club, the music blaring, bodies gyrating on the floor, and people standing around watching as others came in the door.

Is this how her mother met her father? Is this how they came together to create two children before he decided he had all the family time he could handle?

As she walked through the room, twice someone stepped up and asked her to dance, and she continued on. Searching for the man she would have a hard time pretending to like. The urge to kill him on sight was strong, but that would only get her in trouble.

All her training she needed to remember and put to use, or he would see right through her and realize she hated his guts.

The heels she had on were tough to walk in, and she would not be able to run in them. They completed the look that had Detective Baby Daddy eating up the sight of her. Strange, but she almost enjoyed the way he gazed at her like she was dessert on a stick.

Almost to the bar, she spotted him talking animatedly to a man. Was he offering the services of his girls?

When she reached the drink stand, she pushed her way between the bodies until she stood in his line of sight. Then she pretended not to notice him. With a tilt of her head, she leaned down to her chest, and said, "He's here."

With the music pounding, she hoped they could hear her. She felt the touch of his hand before she heard his voice as a shiver rippled through her.

"Hey, baby, you are so hot in pink," he whispered against her ear.

Whirling around, she stared into his cold eyes, thinking she would burn this dress once this was over. "We know each other, love?"

"The other night in the bar, when I had to leave suddenly," he said. "I've thought of you every day and regretted not getting your number."

With a half-lid glance, she said, "Oh yeah, now I remember, you had some outstanding parking tickets."

A laugh came from the burly man. "Oh yes."

How long did she need to play this cat and mouse game with him before she convinced him to go outside with her and they would capture him? The sooner this was over and this creep was behind bars, the better.

His lips touched her bare shoulder and a shudder rippled through her. "Oh, you like that."

Hell, no, she didn't like it. If only she could tell him that was a ripple of disgust, not pleasure. How many women had he conned?

"Let me buy you a drink," he said. "Bartender, two scotch and waters."

"What if I don't like scotch and water?"

He grinned "I'll drink them both, but you're going to love this one. It's the finest scotch and is known for making a girl take her clothes off."

Like that would happen. Like an actress, she needed to entice him out the door. She turned and placed her hand on his chest. "Oh, baby, now that sounds like fun."

The bartender handed him the drinks, and he quickly paid him in cash. He gave her a glass and took his. Staring at her, he smiled. "To getting to know each other very well."

They clinked their glasses together, and she took a tiny sip, fearful something would be in her drink.

"Come on, honey, taste the scotch. You're going to like it," he said. "The liquor goes down real warm and makes you feel so good."

Surprisingly, he was right. A warmth began to fill her, and she set the glass down on the bar afraid of drinking much more. "Come on, let's dance."

Like an octopus, he wrapped his arms around her, and handed the drink to her once more. "Have another taste, and we'll dance all the way to my place."

"Oh, I like the sounds of that," she said, taking another sip. But he waited for her. Knowing her crew would pounce on his ass as soon as they walked out, she went ahead and swallowed a bit more. With the wire and listening in, the guys knew what she had to do. And she wanted to get him out of here, so he would be arrested.

"Let's go," he said, and relief spread through her. Almost over.

Taking her by the hand, he led her out the door. "Where are we going," she asked, wanting his address on record, but he was cagey.

After being in the hot club, the cool night air was soothing against her skin. The lights from the buildings downtown hid the stars, but they had plenty of light as they walked across the lot.

Any moment now they would be jumping out screaming police. Where were they?

"You'll see. I have a little flat in downtown I use."

"A flat," she said. "Where is it?"

"Come on, I'll show you," he said and took her down the street.

Where the fuck was her backup? When they reached the parking lot, they should have taken him down, but no sign of Antonio or the rookie FBI agent.

Now they were headed down Commerce.

"Are we walking?"

"Why not," he said. "I don't live far."

What if something happened to Antonio. Where was her help?

This man did horrible atrocities to women. She didn't want to be alone with him. By golly, if it reached that point, she would fight him to the death.

Panic began to set in, and she tried to reassure herself she knew karate. With a black belt in the martial arts, she could kick this guy's ass if she had to.

But her brain was starting slow and become a little fuzzy and her legs were like sponge.

They promised to be there. Where was Antonio? The cavalry needed to arrive and soon or she would pass out.

CHAPTER 20

*D*amn that arrogant FBI agent who didn't even consider Katherine's life. All he was interested in was capturing Mateo and getting his next promotion. But no, he insisted they wait until Mateo went into the building to determine which apartment was his.

Why hadn't he warned Katherine. Now she would believe he made this decision.

As they walked down the street, he kept his eyes on them, and she appeared to be a little wobbly in those heels. They would soon walk out of his sight, and he couldn't let her disappear.

The couple stopped in front of a building and Mateo glanced up and down the road, before he continued down to the next structure. Stepping out of the car, Antonio used all his tricks to stay hidden from view while racing toward Katherine.

Mateo took Katherine by the hand and guided her up the steps. Why wasn't she resisting?

The stupid FBI agent had gone around to the alley just in case Mateo tried to escape out the back. First, they had to determine where he was going.

Antonio knew he had to hurry as he all but ran down the

sidewalk toward the two of them. Mateo pulled the door open, and they disappeared inside the building. Running, he bound up the steps and yanked on the door. Locked.

He rang the buzzer, nothing. Finally, someone answered. "Yes?"

"Delivery," he lied.

Someone buzzed the door, and he dashed in, trying to locate a directory anything that would help him find Katherine. Standing inside a warehouse building converted into apartments, the elevators and stairs were across from him. The tenants guide next to the door.

His heart raced in his chest like he was running a marathon and yet there was no listing with Mateo's name on it.

A crash and the sound of a woman's raised voice came from the second floor, and he bounded up the stairs searching for where the noise came from.

"Katherine," he screamed.

"Stop," she cried.

That was her voice, but which apartment. Placing his ear next to the door, he heard loud muffled voices inside. "Open up, police."

Nothing. In fact, the building grew quiet, and he became afraid. Bracing against the door, he slammed into it with his shoulder. Nothing. Finally, he pulled out his Glock and fired at the lock, the wood splintering enough to kick in the door the rest of the way.

Peering into the darkness of the apartment, he entered and saw Katherine on the ground. Suddenly, he was knocked from behind to his knees, and he whirled around just as the man slipped through the open door. Raising his gun, he fired a shot, but clearly missed him.

Yanking his radio out, he glanced around, praying they were alone. "He's loose. Headed toward the street."

Damn the FBI agent for being in the alley because now they

had no one to stop him.

Katherine lay sprawled on the floor. Her wrists tied and stretched above her head. A rag stuffed in her mouth with tape across it. Dear God, if he had been any later, she could have been raped.

She moaned like she was in pain, but before he untied her, he needed to make certain they were the only ones in the apartment. With his heart pounding, he walked through checking every room, turning on lights as he went. Finally, when he got to the last room, he concluded they were alone.

Hurrying back to Katherine, she pressed her legs together and she moaned.

As he worked to remove the gag, she sighed a deep heavy breath, like a whimper.

When he managed to free the rag, she sat up and licked her lips. "Are you all right?"

"No, oh dear God, I need you."

What was she talking about? Ignoring her, he began to untie her wrists. When her arms were loose, she wrapped them around his head and pulled his lips to hers.

Surprised that she explored his mouth with her kiss, all he could do was sit there shocked at how much he enjoyed the pressing of her lips. The way her tongue caressed his mouth and the way she sucked his bottom lip. The woman could kiss. But what brought this on?

Did she no longer hate him?

Her hands skimmed down his pants and grasped his buttocks, pulling him in tightly against her, grinding her pelvis against his hips. Finally, he had to know.

With his hands, he pushed back, his breathing harsh. "What are you doing? Did he give you something to drink?"

"Oh yes, I need to get f--"

"Whoa." What did he do now? The woman was coming on to him in ways he'd never considered, and he liked it.

NAILING THE SINGLE DAD

"No, Katherine, you hate me," he reminded her.

A frown crossed her face, her expression shocked as she tried to determine if his comment was true. "No, I don't hate you. Right now, I want you so badly, I can hardly stand it."

"There must have been something in your drink," he said, trying to pull her to her feet. Like a rag doll, she wobbled in her heels.

"How much alcohol did you have?" he asked her, and she leaned down and placed her lips on his neck, kissing him in that special spot that drove him wild.

"Mateo kept saying drink up. Once I finished half a glass, we left. I thought you would be out in the parking lot ready to rescue me," she said, pressing against him.

His cock sprang to attention and the urge to take her on the table was tempting. The last time he had sex was the night before his wife died. No one since her death.

All he wanted now was to bend Katherine over the table and for them to do it in the middle of a crime investigation scene. Not good.

"We need to get you to the car," he said, his breathing raspy. His voice sounded strained even to his ears. "I don't want the patrolmen to see you in this state."

"Then satisfy this urge," she said. "You could make me feel so good."

"And you would hate me even more in the morning. Don't you realize they gave you something? Your drink had to be spiked. Because you have called me every dirty name in the book since you've known me."

She slipped her hand inside his shirt and let her fingers scrape his chest like liquid fire trailing down him. "Katherine."

"See, I knew you liked me," she purred in his ear.

"There's a bed in the corner," she said, her tongue leaving a hot trail across his earlobe that sent a shiver racing through him.

"The patrolmen will be here any minute. Do you want them to

find you naked with me pounding into you?" Because once he started, he would not be able to stop.

A giggle came from her. "They can join in the fun."

Now he was certain she was totally whacked out on some kind of date rape drug. Probably GHB or liquid ecstasy, but whatever Mateo gave her, there would be no sex tonight.

Though now she had raised the idea in his mind, he pictured her naked in his bed, staring up at him while he plunged deep inside her. The very thought had him asking what was wrong with him that he would consider having sex with the woman who hated him.

"Come on," he said, removing her hands, hoping she didn't realize how hard he was. How if she touched him, he would explode and both of them would be embarrassed.

Taking a hold of her arm, he led her out the door, just as the uniformed officers scurried in. "Detective Antonio?"

"Yes, I'm putting Miss McKenzie in my car to wait while we go over the details."

Should he call her an ambulance? Some club drugs one could die from, but she seemed stable at the moment. How long did the effects of the drug last?

The temptation to take her home and spend the night with her stung him, but his daughter was there. And he had never brought another woman into the house before.

When they reached the car, she leaned down and layered her lips over his, kissing him until he pulled her tightly in his arms and returned the kiss.

This time he took control. This time he swept her mouth with his tongue, his heart pounding in his chest as he pushed into her, letting her experience every hard inch of him.

No, they would probably never have sex. Definitely not tonight while she was under the influence of some kind of drug, but she tasted like heaven and the rush of passion that overwhelmed him amazed him. Why was he reacting to Katherine?

CHAPTER 21

When they reached her apartment, he knew she didn't want him to leave. What if she died because of this supposed drug? Yet he couldn't go inside because if he did, there was a good chance they would have sex.

"Maybe I shouldn't go to the door."

"Like hell, you're coming in."

"Can't," he said, shaking his head. "I should go home."

If they did the deed, it would do nothing but create even more problems between them. Yes, he wanted her so badly and the drug left her needing any male body.

As she opened the car door, he went over and helped her out, fearful of her falling. Stumbling, she clung to him as she pressed her body against his. Whatever Mateo gave her had affected his strong, kick ass woman, who purred more like a pussycat right now.

"Give me your door keys," he demanded.

With a smile, she handed them to him, draping herself against him, pressing her breasts into his back as he unlocked the door. But he stayed outside.

"Come in," she told him, trying to pull him inside. "If you

don't, I'm going to undress right here in the door and give the neighbors a bird's eye view."

"Katherine, there are drugs in your system making you say and do these things. We have to work together. In the morning, you will hate me once again," he said, knowing it was true. Though, he still didn't understand why.

"That's not what I want. It's been years since I've had a strong man in my bed. All this time, I've waited, but now I choose you. Close the door, Antonio. You know you want to."

Oh, what was he going to do? The woman intrigued him, she was beautiful, and how could a man not desire a woman like Katherine? Then again, she would make his life a living hell if he slept with her.

Somehow he had to resist her, even though it was hard as he stepped inside and closed the door, determined to make certain she would be all right. She pressed herself against his rock-solid dick. The poor guy was the judge of a tennis match and his head kept swinging back and forth to see who would win.

Leading him by the hand, she took him in the bedroom, and he groaned. How much more temptation could he stand? Just as he made his way to leave, she stood in front of the doorway, trapped.

"Antonio, you sent me flowers. Though we act like we hate each other, I think you really do like me."

What did he say? His daughter sent those flowers with the gushy card. How she even knew Katherine, he didn't know, but he did explain to her he didn't send the roses. And she had been gracious about the mix up.

"Not like this, Katherine," he said. "If we have sex, I want you fully aware of who you're having it with and because we both can't keep our hands off one another. Not because roofies have control of you."

"Every day we could die. Every day could be our last. This is what I want. Tonight. Now either do me or get the hell out of my apartment, so I can go find a man who will."

No, there would not be any other man. Not what he wanted at all. Yet, he did want Katherine. But this was not how he wanted to remember their first time.

Slowly she peeled the hot pink dress down her body, revealing her sweet luscious breasts, her lean stomach and well-defined ribs. All the way down to her feet as his eyes stared at the only thing remaining, her thong. It was strips of material holding up a triangle with a long piece of dental floss keeping everything in place.

Better than any stripper, she removed the thong and she stood there naked. The sight took his breath away and did nothing for the hard-on he was trying to control.

A low groan escaped his chest. How could he walk out? How could he deny himself what she offered?

Her long trim legs were smooth and beautiful, and the high heels accentuated it all. "Do you still want to leave?"

No, he didn't want to go anywhere, but the smarter head between his ears kept warning him to step away. Either way, he would be in trouble with Katherine once the drugs wore off.

How did he respond? "No. Yes."

Like a siren, she wrapped her naked body around him, and he groaned. With a laugh, she said, "Did that help make your decision?"

A good man would turn and walk away. A good man would know that she would be so mad in the morning. A good man...oh hell, he was tired of being good. All his life he'd been good and tonight, he wanted to be so very, very bad with this woman.

Quickly he yanked out his phone and hit the record button, keeping the camera on her face. "Say what you just told me. Because tomorrow, you're going to hate me."

"No, I won't hate you. Now hurry, you've kept me waiting long enough," she said.

"You're under the influence of a drug," he said. "And I doubt you have any recollection of any of this in the morning."

"Would you please put the phone down and fuck me."

A groan escaped from deep within him as he stopped the recording and tossed his phone aside. Thank goodness, Mrs. Langford was staying with Emma. "Just remember that you wanted this. Just remember I tried to tell you no."

She laughed and suddenly he couldn't wait to be inside her.

Hurriedly, she began to unbutton his shirt, her fingers tugging at his clothing in her rapid haste to undress him. As he helped her with his belt buckle, she yanked on his pants, pulling down his underwear, and his hard on sprang out.

"Oh yes, you do want me," she said with a laugh.

He kicked off his shoes and she removed his socks. Leaving him naked and vulnerable to her touch.

With no hesitation, she moved her hands down his warm skin. Eagerly she touched him all over, and he wanted her to caress him. He needed to feel her smooth satiny flesh against his.

Never had he felt this urgent need, like he was the one with ecstasy running through his veins. The sense he would go up in flames at any moment.

Her breathing sounded harsh to his ears, like she couldn't get enough air and that worried him.

With a tug, she placed his fingers to her womanly folds, letting him know what she wanted as he slowly teased her. "Antonio!"

"Oh God, yes," he said as he kissed her. Years had passed since he experienced a woman's touch. Years. With a push, she landed naked on the bed and he kissed his way down her body until he reached her center.

When his lips closed over her, she moaned, tossing and turning beneath his touch. The feel of her fingers tangled in his hair as she clasped his head didn't stop him. He lifted her hips until his mouth was firmly planted where he wanted, and his tongue danced the most erotic tango over her flesh.

While she clutched the bedspread in her fists, she screamed as she began to climax. "Antonio!"

Gently he bit her, bringing her to another climax before she collapsed.

For a moment, they lay there and then she seemed to wilt before his eyes. She rolled over to her side and promptly fell asleep.

A flood of emotions tore through Antonio. Disappointment, hurt, relief, and regret. Once he finally agreed to having sex with her, he was saddened that nothing happened. While waiting was for the best for her, it left him with a raging hard-on and reeling with discouragement.

Yes, all evening he kept saying to wait, but now that he was ready, it was a huge letdown. But how would she react in the morning? Because he wouldn't risk letting her stay alone tonight for fear she would awaken either sick or in desperate need again.

CHAPTER 22

Sunshine beamed through her curtained window causing the pounding behind her eyes to hurt even worse. With a moan, she rolled over, hitting a naked body. With a gasp, she opened her eyes and looked down noticing she was bare as a newborn babe. Sitting up in bed, the motion caused her stomach to roil, and for a moment, she thought she was going to be sick.

Who could she have brought home? With a glance, she peered at the man lying on his side. Detective Dickhead. What the hell was he doing here in her bed naked?

With her head pounding, she tried to remember everything from last night, but gaping holes existed. A sting operation in a bar to capture Mateo, and she remembered walking down the street. After, that her mind was blank.

Lifting the sheet, she stared at him. Dear God, he was naked. His fine ass, rippled back muscles and if only he wasn't lying on his stomach, she could see even more of him.

But why was he here?

"Good morning," he said groggily. "Are you feeling better?"

He rolled over and faced her, his hair rumpled, but he looked great in her bed. Quickly she pulled the covers up high to cover her breasts.

"What happened last night? Why are we in bed together, naked."

Whatever occurred, she prayed they didn't have sex. The thought of sleeping with her enemy made her so frustrated. Why would she agree to that?

With a toss of his head, he groaned. "I warned you, but you refused to listen to me."

"About what?" she asked her temper rising. "What are you doing in my bed?"

This morning, a little soreness existed between her legs. No, they couldn't. Just no.

The man sighed. "Working the case, when you went into the bar, did Mateo buy you a drink. Do you remember?"

"Yes," she said. "And I tried to sip the beverage, because I feared it was spiked."

"You did drink some."

"Of course," she said. "While I sipped, he would encourage me to drink more."

The memory of him urging her to bottom up suddenly slammed into her, and she cringed at the thought of what she'd done. What if Antonio had not rescued her.

"Either Mateo or the bartender must have slipped GHB or liquid ecstasy in your glass. A common date rape drug. It makes you supercharged sexually and you can't resist. Can you remember experiencing anything like that?"

For a moment, she closed her eyes, the feelings of being in another world coming over her. The way she stumbled in her heels and Mateo smiling at her like she was fresh candy. His for the taking.

"My body was burning and felt weak. When you touched me, there was an explosion of need."

Oh, no, what happened? Who did she have sex with?

"As we walked down the street, I kept looking for you and thinking, if he got me alone, I would be powerless to stop him. All I wanted was to find you," she said. "Where the hell were you?"

They were supposed to grab him in the parking lot, and somehow, she wound up in his apartment so afraid. At least that was what she remembered.

"That young FBI agent thought we should try to locate Mateo's apartment, he wouldn't let me go after you until the two of you were inside. Once you were in the building, I had the hardest time finding you, until you screamed."

The foggy image of Mateo tying her up and her threatening to kick his ass, her limbs not moving correctly, felt like a slow dance machine. But other than that, she didn't remember many details. Her body seemed lethargic, yet the slightest touch left her needy and wanting. And then everything went black.

"So why are you here in my bed, naked?" she asked. "How did we get here?"

A grin spread across his face. "First you pulled me into your apartment and repeated over and over you wanted sex. Next, you stripped off your clothes and begged me."

No, there is no way she would beg him. No way she would beseech any man for anything.

"No way, you are such a lying Baby Daddy," she said. "Never would I plead with any man for sex. And I would never invite you into my apartment."

"Last night, I kept telling you, you would hate me in the morning and you didn't believe me. So I recorded you. Because I wanted to make certain you didn't try to affix something on me."

Oh, dear, what did he record? Oh, no, now she had to see the video.

"What I'm going to pin on you are the parts of your phone after I destroy it. Now show me what you got."

The man sat up in her bed and reached over and picked up his phone and then played a video showing her begging him to have sex with her. That she needed him while he tried to convince her she will hate him in the morning, if they do this, and she just laughed at him. Laughed.

"Stop, I've seen enough," she said, lying down, trying to absorb the fact she made love to Antonio. That she begged him to do her. Tears welled up in her eyes, but she refused to cry in front of him. "How could that happen when I don't remember a thing."

Of all the humiliating things to take place, never in her life had something like this happened.

He grinned and scooted closer to her. "This morning, I planned to wake you and tell you we had sex, but I can't. That would be too mean. Keep in mind, there is only so much a man can take before he agrees. After I finally gave up, you achieved orgasm, and then you passed out on me."

Like a bomb, her mouth dropped open. "You gave me an orgasm, but we didn't have sex?"

"Yes."

There were only two ways that could happen...foreplay or oral intercourse. Either way, her cheeks burned with color. "How?"

To be prepared for the worst, she needed to learn all the details, even the most embarrassing ones.

A chuckle came from his chest. "Are you sure you want to know?"

"Yes," she whispered as she rolled over and leaned on her elbow. "Complete my utter humiliation. I must know everything."

Tears came to her eyes. How could she face anyone ever again?

"Are you certain you want to hear this?"

"Get on with it."

"After you stripped off my clothes, you let me know exactly how you liked your foreplay, by taking my fingers and placing them where you wanted them to go. Then I went down on you," he said. "We know each other very intimately now."

Dear God, she had never been more embarrassed in her life. "What happened afterward that we didn't finish what we'd started?"

"After you had your orgasm, you passed out. Since there is a dangerous chance of you throwing up and aspirating, no way I would leave you alone. So I spooned you most of the night."

"You did what?"

Could this day become any worse? To wake naked next to the man she hated and learned she begged him to have sex with her and eventually he gave her oral sex before she passed out.

"We slept curled around each other all night," he said and winked at her. "Nice body you got there."

That was it. Her embarrassment was complete. She sat up in bed, grabbing the sheet before it dropped exposing her breasts. "Get out. Now. Go, so I can die alone."

A smile graced his face as he shook his head. "Suck it up. Not much happened after that, except you fell asleep. Until I was sure you were all right, I stayed here and watched you sleep."

It was sweet of him to make sure she didn't die, but right now, she was dying with the telling of what transpired last night. Oh, my, how did she face this man and work with him every day when they had done such intimate acts?

"Oh, you should have gone home," she said, sitting up staring at him. "How is it going to look when you walk out of my apartment this morning?"

With a toss of the covers, he grabbed his underwear off the floor and pulled them on before she saw him. Dang, he'd seen everything, why didn't she get a chance.

"Your neighbors will smile and say, 'Oh look, Katherine finally has a boyfriend. She's not going to be a lonely cat woman after all.'"

The man deliberately irritated her and was doing a fine job of just making her madder. "No, they're going to wonder why I chose you."

"Honey, you did choose me, last night. Do you need to see the video again, where you were begging? I'm a good guy because you had an orgasm and I didn't."

Maybe he had a point, but that didn't mean she wanted to hear it at this moment. In fact, none of this seemed real.

A sarcastic laugh escaped from her. "Don't expect me to feel sorry for you. Poor thing has to go home all frustrated. Now you understand how most women feel after sex. Frustrated."

As he stood, he yanked up his pants and put his shirt on. Once he stuffed the hem down inside his jeans, he turned to her as he finished dressing. With the sheet wrapped around her, she got out of bed, trying to keep herself covered.

At the door, he pulled her to him and kissed her, shocking her. The kiss was intense as his lips claimed hers, his tongue sweeping the inside of her mouth, consuming hers.

Abruptly he released her. "Obviously, you've been sleeping with the wrong men if they left you frustrated. Last night after your second orgasm, you fell fast asleep. Completely satisfied. Sated. See you at the office in two hours."

Speechless, she watched him walk out the door and wanted to scream with annoyance. No, she couldn't enjoy Detective Baby Daddy's kiss and now she wished she remembered the orgasm he gave her.

CHAPTER 23

Katherine walked into the office, needing to talk to someone, anyone about how she needed off this case and now. Why had she let him kiss her this morning? And she liked the kiss and that scared her more than anything. When his lips moved over hers, it felt like they belonged there.

No, she would never get involved with a man she considered to be a baby daddy. No, just no. Time to excuse herself from this investigation.

The office reeked of silence. This place was never this quiet. Either the phone was ringing or Gina chased the cat or Merlin knocked something over or Brittany and Jennifer were talking.

The memory of how last time she caught Gina and her Uncle Sam slammed into her. Oh, no, not today. The sound of Gina screaming Big Daddy would send her into orbit. Especially after what happened last night.

"Where is everyone?" she yelled.

Gina walked out of her Uncle Sam's office giggling, her cheeks rosier than usual, her lipstick smeared. Oh, good grief. But the worst part, her skirt was rolled up in her panties. Couldn't the woman feel that?

"Morning, you're up bright and early this fine day," she said.

Fine day, her ass. Today sucked and this made everything worse. "Pull down your skirt. It's stuck in your damn underwear."

With a laugh, Gina hurriedly pulled the skirt into place. "Oh my."

"Everyone knows you're doing my uncle."

The woman shrugged like she didn't care. "Why would you want to be involved with that old fart? He's been married five times. Obviously, he doesn't know how to get it right."

If after two attempts at marriage and it didn't work, she would buy herself a cat and a vibrator and be done with men.

"Oh, honey, I've said I do three times. At some point, you think what's one more. Besides who said I wanted to marry him? Oh, I do enjoy playing slap and tickle with him."

"How about not on office time," Katherine said, feeling really cranky.

"We're in a fine mood this morning," Gina said, dodging her comment.

"You wouldn't be so great either if some man slipped you a date rape drug," she said ready to fight everyone at the moment.

This was why she became a counselor, to learn how to control her emotions better and train others. Currently, they were in full unleash mode and someone was going to experience her wrath.

"What the hell is going on?" Jennifer said, walking in the door.

"Katherine is spitting mad because some man slipped her a Special K last night," Gina said. "If she got a little, occasionally, she wouldn't be so strung out."

That just went all over Katherine. How could the woman compare being raped with sex? Someone needed an ass whooping this morning, and she would be more than happy to oblige.

"Whoa," Gina said. "I'm not saying rape is a good thing. It is a violent, horrible act. Any man who commits crimes against women deserves his tally whacker cut off. Face it, you need a man to smooth out the rough edges. Someone to hold you and love you."

Right now, she'd settle for coffee and a long talk to someone who cared. Not Gina.

"You weren't raped last night," Jennifer asked, her face frightened.

"No, Antonio saved me," she said. "We need a conference. I need off this case."

"That Antonio is such a nice man. I'd let him into my bed anytime," Gina said, smiling, which only upset Katherine even more.

The thought of him sleeping with anyone left her cringing inside. She didn't like being this way. She didn't want to be attracted to the hot detective.

"Gina, go away before I kick your ass," Katherine said "One more word is all it will take."

The older woman huffed off to the kitchen. "Merlin."

"Come into the office and let's talk," Jennifer said. As soon as she closed the door, she turned on Katherine. "What happened?"

For the next five minutes, she poured her heart out to Jennifer, telling her how Mateo slipped her the drugs in the alcohol and how Antonio saved her. Then she confessed to what occurred this morning when she woke up naked in bed beside him.

"I can't work with him anymore," she said. "I just can't."

Jennifer sat back and started laughing. "I'm sorry. This is not funny, but the thought of some man giving you not one but two fantastic orgasms and not taking any for himself. That's hysterical and you fell asleep."

"No, it is not funny. The whole thing is rather embarrassing. How do I face him again? When he left, he kissed me."

"Did you like his kiss?"

What could she say? The earth moved with that kiss. Bands and harps were playing in harmony with angels singing. The man rocked her world, and she had stood there like a lump on a stone, not moving.

A deep sigh escaped her. "Of course, I did. It was a kiss to remember. But he's a baby daddy."

"Maybe he's changed. Maybe he's different now that he's older."

"No, baby daddies seldom evolved into nice men. They continued spreading their seed to as many women as possible."

"What if he's not. What if he's like my father? What if one day he said to me *I'm tired of being a family man and don't want to be married any longer?*"

"Then you would have to deal with a divorce like your mother and all the other women have done," Jennifer said. "Antonio's boss specifically requested you for the job. You have to see this through."

Not the news Katherine wanted to hear, but she knew her cousin was right. This morning, she considered going to Kevin Harris and telling him they could no longer work together on this case, but knew that was the chicken-shit way out.

Suddenly Jennifer's face grew pale. "Oh no. Here it comes."

"What?"

She bent over the trash can and vomited.

"Are you certain you're not pregnant?"

Her cousin leaned back against the chair. "No, I'm not certain of anything. No, I'm not ready."

"Time to man up. By golly, I'm going to help you," Katherine said and walked out the door.

Thirty minutes later, she walked in and handed Jennifer a small purple box. "Here, take the damn pregnancy test."

CHAPTER 24

Antonio strolled into the office smiling and whistling. Last night had been stressful, but waking up with Katherine beside him, he felt great. No, they hadn't done the deed yet, but after the kiss they shared this morning, things were looking up and it wouldn't be long now.

The idea of making love to the woman he once considered his arch enemy was nerve racking. Maybe all this hostility between them was pent up passion, but whatever reason she called him names, he planned on getting to the bottom of it.

Time for an honest-to-goodness no-holds-barred discussion and this time he wanted answers. This time he wanted to find out the reason why she called him a baby daddy when all he had was a beloved adopted daughter.

"My office," his boss said.

The tone of his voice sounded serious, but what could the man be upset about. The case was going slower than expected but they had saved not one, but two girls, and almost caught Mateo last night.

The two men entered his office and a young Hispanic man sat

in a chair, staring off like he carried the world on his shoulders. He glanced up once they walked into the room.

"Antonio, I'd like you to meet Tomas Castano. Tomas, this is the detective working on the case. Tell him what you came to me about today."

The man sighed. "I'm afraid for my life and my girlfriend and our unborn baby. My cousin is Mateo Torres."

A trickle of unease wound down Antonio's spine. Why would he come to the police? Was this a setup for failure or was he trying to get information?

"When my girlfriend became pregnant, we were both scared. Mateo told me not to worry, he would handle everything, including the doctor bills. Madison—Madison Johnson's her name—is now almost nine months and I haven't been able to see her for the last month. They refuse to let me talk to her, see her, or tell her I want our child."

Why did this sound familiar? Oh, how he wished they would find the new location of where the women had been taken, so they could rescue them.

"What happened?"

"Mateo took her off to a place he said where she could have the baby, but I want to tell her that's our child. That I want us to get married and raise this baby we created together."

"Do you know where they took her?"

"It's a house with several pregnant girls living together. They gave me an address, but they're no longer there."

Yes, this sounded more and more like what transpired with Isabella and Olivia.

"What does Mateo say when you ask about her?"

The kid acted nervous and that made Antonio a little suspicious. His words said one thing, but his body language didn't match.

"He tells me she is busy creating a child and she says she

doesn't want anything to do with me any longer. I don't believe this. We were talking of going away together."

The poor guy probably walked right into Mateo's trap and now his girlfriend and baby were part of the black-market adoption agency.

"How old is Madison?"

"She just turned nineteen."

"Does her family know where she is and that she's pregnant?"

"No, in fact, I contacted her mother, but she refused to speak to me. Finally, I decided to come here. I'm worried about her. My cousin is known for being in illegal activities. He'll kill me if he learns that I came here."

The first step would be to talk to Madison's mother and father to find out if they know where their daughter was.

"When was the last time you had any contact with her?"

"Two months ago," he said. "I've written letters, called and tried to see her, but nothing. Last night, I overheard one of the men saying the girls were moved to 931 West Georgia Boulevard. But when I went by, the place looked dark."

That was the previous location where they picked up Ms. Smith. "Hang on a minute."

Getting up, Antonio went into his office and found his file on the case. While they waited on him, he glanced back through his notes from Isabella and Olivia. A list of names. And yes, Madison was listed by both Olivia and Isabella that she was being held. If he told the man, it would confirm the girls talked and put them in jeopardy. What if Tomas worked for Mateo?

"I'm sorry, I thought I had some information on that address, but I don't," he said.

The two men gazed at each other. "Give me your cell number and we have any further questions, I'll contact you. Or if you remember anything else about where the house might be located."

The temptation to tell him they broke up one house was

strong, but Antonio remained silent. The less the kid knew, the better. Because he didn't trust which side Tomas was on just yet. Or it could be like he said.

The boy stood. "Look, I'm young, we should have waited. But I want to protect Madison and our child. I want to be there when the baby is born. Please help me find them."

The young man was almost crying, and Antonio's heart ached for the young man if what he said was true. Though he never had the chance to have his own kid, he wanted one.

Even now, it was tempting to think about finding someone and having a child and then he would remember Sheila and what happened to her. At any moment, that could be him.

The anguish he'd gone through at her death was enough to make him realize he would never do that to someone else. The image of Katherine came to mind and with sadness, he realized he should cool things down before they became involved. Before they had sex.

After the boy left the room, his captain stared at him. "What the hell is this Mateo guy doing? I thought he was into sex trafficking, but now his operation has expanded and he's running a damn black-market adoption agency. We need to catch him and take him off the streets."

How did you tell someone you were working with, they needed to dial things back a bit? Especially when it had just heated up. This was why he never got involved in an office romance.

"Agreed and we're doing the best we can to find him. We've rescued two girls, but there are more."

"What the hell happened last night? Is Katherine all right?"

The news had spread through the precinct that the FBI got a little too greedy and jeopardized a civilian helping out.

"She's fine, no thanks to that young agent Chad assigned us. If we followed the plan, Mateo would be behind bars and we wouldn't have needed to rescue Katherine. They wanted to locate his apartment, hoping he ran his business from that location.

"The man is not going to take a woman where he's running his illegal operation unless he trusts her. The whole job was botched because of the greediness of the FBI."

"You going to put that in your report?"

How he would like to send a reprimand to the agent's superior to inform him how reckless and stupid the young man was with other people's lives. No matter what he decided, he would not dismiss how they didn't capture Mateo because of his irresponsible greed.

With a sigh, Antonio said, "My report will be worded differently, but I will lay the blame on them."

His captain chuckled. "Speaking of, here comes our bounty hunter queen now. She went into your office."

As Antonio entered the room, he could tell she flipped off his boss, who had his back to them. She was in one hell of mood and yet he understood. Last night had been dangerous and they should have settled for getting this creep off the streets. And without their stupid move, his evening would not have been rescuing Katherine from herself.

"Well, I can tell your state of mind has certainly improved," he said. "Don't blame Kevin, blame that asshole Chad sent with us."

"No, it hasn't. In fact, let's just say the morning went downhill after you left."

That didn't sound good, but it left him curious.

"Shame, I wasn't there to make you feel better," he said teasing her.

She gave him a look that said to clearly back off. "Let's work to end this case. Too many young girls are being hurt and this guy Mateo needs to spend some time locked behind bars."

"Agreed. Now let me tell you the latest developments. Then we're going to search for Madison Johnson, nineteen years old, nearly nine months pregnant with Tomas Castano's child, cousin to Mateo."

After he told her everything he knew, she frowned. "Do you think it was a setup?"

"Don't know, but one of the girls is named Madison that we're searching for. My fear is Mr. Castano was sent to learn if we would share our information. Sometimes when the Feds are closing in, they decide time to move the operation. Let's find those girls."

"Well, Mr. Baby Daddy will have to wait."

CHAPTER 25

This afternoon, she sat once again with the girls listening to their problems, her mind drifting off to poor Madison Johnson who unbeknownst to her boyfriend fell into Mateo's trap. While she wanted to believe Tomas, he was kind to Mateo.

Today, almost everyone had spoken except for a young girl named Ashley. A beautiful girl the same age as Emma, shy and somewhat reserved and very seldom spoke.

Five minutes were left in the session and then Katherine would bring their time to a close and hide out until Emma and her father drove away. The last person she needed to see was Antonio.

After what took place the other night, she would never forget what he said they did. And yet the rational part of her wondered if what he said really happened. She still had no memories of what occurred that night.

"My mother's boyfriend cornered me in the kitchen and told me if I made his life hell, he'd get rid of me," Ashley blurted out.

At twelve years of age, the young girl would someday be a beauty with her long dark hair and big green eyes.

Katherine jerked to attention and the other counselor also went into high alert. "Did he say what he would do?"

"No," Ashley said. "I don't like him, so I avoid him."

"What does your mother say?"

"Mom thinks I want her and daddy to get back together. Honestly, I just want to be alone. I don't like Mateo," she said.

Katherine's heart leapt out of her chest, and for a moment, she couldn't believe her source of good luck. "How often does she see him?"

Could this be the same Mateo or a different man?

The little girl shrugged. "Almost every weekend. Saturday night he was busy, and he didn't visit until Sunday."

Saturday night was when they tried to trap Mateo and the FBI screwed things up.

That son of a bitch. Could he be dating one of her girl's mothers? Hardly able to contain herself and focus on the present, she took a deep breath. What a great lead, if it was the Mateo they were searching for. One she hoped and prayed would put him behind bars for years.

But how did she explain how she learned this information without Antonio figuring out she was in his daughter's counseling group. That she was their leader.

Somehow she would come up with an excuse, but first, she must counsel this young girl. "Have you told your mother exactly what he said to you?"

"Yes, and she thinks I didn't understand what he said."

Griminy, how many times did a child have to be abducted before parents started to listen and believe in their children.

The head consultant of the group fiercely wrote notes.

"Here are some things all of you should know. This is a way to protect yourself against any man. Don't be alone in the same room. Keep your phone close by and try to record him. If he continues to bother you, go to your school counselor or tell us, and we will immediately contact the authorities."

"Please don't call the police," Ashley said her eyes widening with fright. "Mamma would be so angry."

"We're not," she reassured her. "What is said in here, stays in here. That being said, your safety is important. You will tell us if things become worse, or he tries anything."

"Yes, I will," she said with a sigh.

Katherine feared for this child. How did she handle keeping her confidence and going after Mateo? Maybe it was a different man. The girl was the perfect age for him to kidnap and it's possible he was using the mother to pick her up.

A sick feeling gathered like a fire pit in her stomach at the thought of him taking Ashley. If women ruled the world, men like him would be dickless.

"All right, let's stand and give each other a hug. Some of you made some progress tonight. Remember, do not let what has happened to you in the past rule your future. Have a wonderful week everyone."

As the girls filed out the door, Pat, the more experienced counselor hung back.

"Do you think we should turn him into the police?"

What could she say? Sure, it could be a different Mateo, but what if it was the same? So far, the man had been too cagey for the law. He managed to stay one step ahead of them. "Let's hear what she says next week. I'm going to go by her home. Possibly do a house call on the mother."

"But you can't repeat what she told us in session tonight," Pat said.

"No, but I can prepare the mother and warn her."

"Just be careful, you're walking a fine line."

She was walking more than that. Once she learned if he was the Mateo they searched for, she would need to explain to Antonio and do so without him realizing how she got this tip.

CHAPTER 26

"Daddy, would you ever date someone who might hurt me?" Emma asked in the car on their way home from her therapy session. The five-o'clock traffic crawled.

What brought this up? This counseling was supposed to be helping her get over her mother being shot and her father being a dick. Why in the world would she question this now?

"No."

"But what if you didn't see what was going on? What if they were doing something that would either harm or threaten me?"

Something was happening that had her questioning this, and he needed to find out. "That's when you would come to me and tell me what was going on. That this person I brought into our home threatened you or harmed you. No one hurts my girl."

Silence filled the vehicle while they wound their way through Dallas, heading for home. Tonight, Antonio wanted a good night's rest so they could begin searching out the location of Madison Johnson and any other missing young women in Mateo's care.

With each girl they captured, they learned more about the others.

"Dad, I do want you to date again, but after listening to several girls this afternoon, I don't know. Our counselor, I really like her, and she's single. The two of you should go out just once."

A horn honked behind him, and he resisted the urge to flip out his badge and show him who he was dealing with.

"Honey, it's been so many years since I went out on a date, I wouldn't know how to act."

"Then time for you to try once again," she said.

"Right now, with work I'm so busy and I'll think about it," he said not wanting to promise her anything and knowing it would never happen. The image of Katherine came to mind, and he quickly pushed her away.

As much as he liked Katherine, they worked together, and besides, she was such a crazy risk taker, she wouldn't be around long. And he could never go through losing his wife again. Never.

"Well, whoever you decide to date, they can't come between us. Ever. And if they threaten to harm or make me disappear, I'll be running to you."

"Wait? Someone said this in your group today?"

"Yes, some girl is afraid of her mother's boyfriend. I can't tell you anymore, but, Daddy, I'm scared for her."

Right in his daughter's counseling group, the threat of violence was like that movie *The Slime*, where this nasty ooze grew and spread across the earth infiltrating everything.

As they pulled up to a red light, he glanced around at the other cars, thinking. How could he put this delicately?

"I realize you can't share what is said in the counseling session. But if someone is in danger, you can always tell me, and I'll make certain they are placed in safety. Or at the very least, your counselor should call the police."

They were trained professionals; they should be cognizant of the laws.

She smiled. "Ms. Wilson, the main therapist sits in the corner taking notes. Today, I noticed her writing lots after this girl spoke. Sometimes I wonder if she even knows what is said. The intern, the one I like, she keeps us in line and makes certain we stay on topic."

"Good," he said.

"Pizza?" she asked and he smiled.

He couldn't resist her. "Pizza it is."

CHAPTER 27

Katherine walked into the agency, and for once, everyone appeared to be in their cubicle or office working. It was quiet. Almost too quiet. Gazing around, she saw Shaggy sitting in his office and knocked on his door. He motioned her in the door and hung up the phone.

"Hey, where you been?"

"Chasing a man named Mateo Torres. What can you tell me?"

Shaggy shook his head. "Not much, except to say he is one mean son of a bitch."

"Can you give me any intelligence on his hideouts, where he hangs or anything I can use?"

A sigh escaped the man who looked more like a drug dealer than a bounty hunter. But his persona on the street always got them excellent information.

"The rumor is he has a stable of women he pimps, but he's into something else. No one is talking, but they say he's raking in the cash. If his profit was from drugs, I wouldn't be surprised, but the rival gangs would take him out. Let me ask some of my sources about him."

After sinking into a chair, she proceeded to give him all the detailed dirt she had on Mateo.

"One of the kids in my counseling group, her mother is dating a man named Mateo. This may or may not be the Mateo I'm looking for, but he warned the girl to behave, or he would have her removed. Currently, he's selling young teen girls to a brothel in Mexico, so I'm afraid for her."

"Damn, this guys a bigger scumbag than I thought."

Katherine was frightened for Ashley, but she couldn't betray her trust. Maybe Shaggy would keep an eye out for her. "Would you mind doing some surveillance work and watching over her at her home?"

"Where does she live?"

She gave him the address and he smiled. "This is not far from where I'm at."

"Good," she said. "Thank you. This one I can't tell Detective Baby Daddy. And I don't want him to learn I'm the intern counselor sitting in and leading the sessions."

Katherine hadn't figured out how she would tell Antonio about this new lead. What if she told him Shaggy heard about this woman dating a man named Mateo? There was no way she would tie the connection to his daughter's therapy group.

Shaggy frowned at her. "The two of you need to have a sit-down conversation and talk about your feelings regarding him. Someone has led you astray. That is all I'm going to say on the subject."

Sitting across from him, Katherine stared at him. "If you know something different, you should tell me."

"Not my circus and not my monkeys. What I will tell you is talk to Jennifer. She's having a rough day."

The memory of delivering her the pregnancy test and telling her to pee on the stick suddenly came rushing back.

"Oh shit," Katherine said. "This morning I bought her a pregnancy test and told her to take the damn thing."

A smile crossed Shaggy's face. "That explains a lot. But she's not happy about something. Go calm her down because she's been throwing things in her office and cursing up a storm."

Typical Jennifer behavior when she was frustrated. Why wasn't she excited? Time to check on her and try to soothe her and learn what Katherine already suspected. She was pregnant.

"All right," Katherine said, rising. "Thanks for helping me."

"After you talk to Jennifer, have a talk with Detective Marino."

That was something she wouldn't promise to him or anyone else. Dang, after waking up beside him, it became harder and harder to call him names. Yes, she knew it was childish, and accepted her name-calling, and frankly, didn't care. One of her many faults people could get over.

In therapy, calling men baby daddies was the result of her own pain. As far as she was concerned, her own father was the biggest baby daddy of them all. There would be no heart-to-heart with the detective.

She walked out the door and Shaggy yelled at her. "Sit down and talk to him, Katherine."

No, just no. Not saying anything to Shaggy, she hurried toward Jennifer's office, hoping to escape from Shaggy pinning her down to a commitment—she couldn't give in.

When she approached Jennifer's door the lights were out and when she cracked the door open, she saw her cousin, head down on her desk sleeping. Funny and yet her tiredness confirmed what Katherine suspected all along. Jennifer was probably pregnant. Some noise had her raising her head and staring bleary-eyed at her.

"You," she said angrily. "Damn you."

"Why what did I do," Katherine said innocently, but she knew. By purchasing the test, she forced Jennifer to face the truth. Sitting across from her, she smiled and asked. "How did the test go?"

"I'm pregnant," she yelled. "Are you satisfied?"

"You're blaming me? Since you met that handsome husband of yours, you're the one fornicating like a rabbit."

When Jennifer hunted Christopher Lopez of the Lopez crime cartel, she had fallen hard for the man's totally legal twin brother Carson. Married in Vegas, the two seemed happy.

Shocked, tears streamed down her face. "Look at me, I'm supposed to be happy and all I can do is cry. I'm thrilled and terrified and this was not when we planned to start a family."

"So your timing is a little off," Katherine said. "The tears could be the hormones."

Pregnancy hormones were working Jennifer and the woman didn't even realize it. Somehow she needed to calm her down.

"Oh shit, you're being way too logical. How am I going to work with a baby? How can I chase bad guys and avoid being killed? There is so much to think about and the biggest thing is I haven't told Carson yet."

That was odd. These two were so in love. Why would she refrain from telling the man she loved they were expecting?

"Why?"

"I've only known for a couple of hours. How do I tell him? Oh, by the way, honey, remember we were going to wait a few *years*? Well, guess what. I'm pregnant now. What if he hates me or the baby?"

Katherine had never seen her cousin so worked up. Carson would love this child, and once she got past her fear, Jennifer would be thrilled over this baby. For now, she was scared.

"Come on, I don't think you're giving him much credit here. Carson, he'll be so excited."

Jennifer's eyes widened and her hand flew to her mouth, and she screamed. "What if it's twins? Oh, dear God, what if we have twins? He's a twin."

Carson's twin brother was killed by his uncle who ran a mafia family before they married.

"Calm down. You'll have help. When are you going to tell him?"

What a wonderful surprise and yet Katherine thought of the case she was working right now. A black-market adoption agency. The ugliness in the world was sometimes a little overwhelming. This child would be the first in a new generation and would be welcomed and loved and pampered.

"We're going out to dinner tonight and I'm going to tell him then."

Her face crumpled again. "My biggest fear is he's going to take one look at my face and realize something is wrong. Nothing is really wrong. I just need some time to adjust to the thought I'm pregnant. Oh, my God, I'm going to have a baby."

How could she not have known? For weeks now, she'd been throwing up but refused to face the fact she was expecting.

"You've suspected for a while. Why didn't you want to face the reality of the situation?"

"Damn you, Katherine. I liked you better before you got this counseling degree. Now all you want to do is psychoanalyze us. Yes, I suspected and kept thinking it would go away."

Tears welled up in her eyes. "This is never going away. For the rest of my life, I'll have a child. Someone depending on me to love and cherish and raise this person to be a good human being. What if I screw up?"

"Everyone screws up," Katherine told her. "Including our parents."

All those years ago, still affected Katherine today, so she understood raising children was serious. The desertion of her father left a hole in their family that, to this day, Katherine tried to fill and found herself wary of men in general.

Jennifer sat, sobbing. "Can't you see I'm happy."

Most certainly. Every crying woman in America was jumping for joy. Not.

"Understand," Katherine said. "Now, I want you to dry your

tears, wipe your face, put on some fresh lipstick and think about your heritage. You come from a long line of women who faced tougher obstacles than having a baby. Then go home to that handsome husband of yours and surprise him. He's going to be excited."

"Yes, I think so. So, in other words, you want me to suck it up and be the woman I'm supposed to be and make the family proud."

"You got it, buttercup," Katherine told her as she stood, walked around her desk and hugged Jennifer. "Actually, I'm a little jealous. And you tell that handsome husband if he turns out to be a baby daddy, I will personally kick his ass."

And she would. No one should ever desert a child for any reason.

"No, I'm sure he'll be thrilled. Not so happy when I tell him I plan on continuing to work," Jennifer said and gave a small smile.

CHAPTER 28

*A*ntonio sat in the unmarked car with Katherine at his side, watching the comings and goings of a house. This was the boring part of detective work. And the woman beside him had been unusually quiet this morning. For a woman who normally would tell him how she felt about things, she seemed more pensive today.

After everything that happened the other night and waking up together, he wanted her back to her normal talking self. He wanted the Katherine with the saucy mouth he discovered was so ripe for kissing.

The outspoken attitude and the woman he never wanted to see hurt again. The other night watching her under the influence of a drug that could have harmed her frightened him. Worried, his chest squeezed tightly. As much as he didn't want to get involved, he cared for this woman.

"Jennifer is pregnant," she said suddenly her voice tense. "I'm happy for her."

"You don't seem very happy."

"On the inside, I'm jubilant and terrified as well."

"But a pregnancy should be a joyous time."

A frown crossed her face and that surprised him.

"What? You don't like babies?"

"No, I want a couple of kids of my own someday, but first, I need to find someone who is not interested in just getting me pregnant and leaving me."

"Is that what you fear for Jennifer?"

She looked at him like he was crazy. "Are you kidding me? That man is nuts about Jennifer, and she's totally smitten with him. But the agency is her life and I'm worried about her working while she's expecting and not wanting to slow down. If she lost this baby, she would be devastated. It's something we're going to all sit down and discuss."

For a moment, she looked pensive, and he realized she was concerned about her cousin and the stress and danger of the job.

"This could happen more and more in our agency. Jennifer is married and Brittany's engaged. Of the three cousins, I'm the only one who is available. There is Shaggy, Jon Paul and Gina, but they're not family."

The way she sounded wistful, kind of surprised him, like she wanted to say I do.

"I'm shocked you want to get married. I thought you believed all men just wanted to be baby daddies."

A laugh came from her. "Of course, you would, you're a baby daddy. No, I want a lasting relationship with the 2.5 kids and the picket white fence and a mother-in-law who loves me."

That brought a rumbling chuckle came from his chest. "The mother-in-law is a little much. The rest sounds reasonable, except why in the hell do you believe I'm a baby daddy? Why? Please tell me because the only daughter I have is Emma, and she's adopted."

Katherine's head swung around to face him, and her mouth dropped open. She stared at him like she'd seen a ghost.

Mateo walked out of the house, a spring to his step and

whistling. With a quick glance around, he got in a beat-up old car.

"He's on the move. We gotta roll."

Antonio started the car and pulled out and began to follow Mateo. Driving down the street, he tried to stay hidden behind several cars, he also didn't want the man too far ahead of him.

"No one is with him," Katherine said, pulling out her Glock and making sure the gun was loaded.

The man headed out of town.

"Maybe he's going to the house where the girls are kept."

"That would be terribly lucky, wouldn't it? I'd be tempted to buy a lottery ticket tonight."

"Can't win if you don't play," Antonio said. "And I don't play."

"Damn it!" Katherine said her voice sounding stringent. "Your daughter is adopted?"

Shocked they were still talking about Emma, he gazed at Katherine. "Yes, she was my wife's child. After we married, I adopted her."

"Son of a bitch," she said, cursing beneath her breath.

Why was she acting all upset and swearing, especially when they needed to be focused on what was going on here and now?

"Would you focus? We have a car following us," Antonio said glancing up in his rearview mirror nervously.

The black SUV pulled around to pass them on the right and as they did, a man rolled down the window and fired a shot, barely missing Katherine. Which sent panic sizzling through him centering in his chest.

"Like hell," she said and returned fire, but she went for his tires not his body. The first bullet hit the front tire and caused a blowout. Immediately the SUV lost control, swerving across the road, going into a spin. The driver tried to bring the vehicle back, but no matter what he did, the car continued to spin.

All the while Antonio did his best to keep his eye on Mateo, but the big, black SUV blocked his line of sight. No way would he go around the man who now rolled the big vehicle blocking the lanes of traffic.

Thankfully, no one was near the crashing vehicle.

Mateo drove on down the highway unscathed while Antonio brought the police car to a halt. Both of them jumped out and ran toward the vehicle, their weapons drawn.

"Out of the car," he demanded.

While he watched the vehicle, he also tried to make certain Katherine was not in danger. The woman was fearless and dangerous, and she had no training with the police department. Being a bounty hunter did not qualify her for special situations like this.

The woman ignored him. Even though he kept motioning for Katherine to stay back, she refused. When he arrived at the passenger's side, a young girl who had been in the back came crawling out under her own power.

"Anyone else in there?"

"Only the driver, who didn't move," she said. "Please help me. They kidnapped me."

Katherine took the girl and led her away from the SUV while Antonio searched the car.

"What's your name?" he heard her ask the young woman.

Peering inside the vehicle, he could see the man, but he wasn't moving. Finally, he crawled in and touched his neck searching for a pulse. Nothing. Dead.

With a sigh he stepped away. Sirens wailed in the distance. If the man had lived, he hoped they could have spoken to him and learned who he worked for, but obviously, that was no longer possible.

CHAPTER 29

Shaking, Katherine led the young woman away from the wreck to the police vehicle.

"Are you all right?" Katherine asked. "You're not hurt or need an ambulance?"

"No, I think I'm all right," she said trembling. "That got very scary when you started firing shots."

Katherine had not seen her in the car. But when the driver fired, she shot back.

"Yes, I'm certain that must have been terrifying," she said.

"What's your name?"

"Haley Williams."

"How old are you?"

"Sixteen," she said, her body trembling.

"Did they hurt or rape you?"

"No, I'm just scared. Please help me get away from them," she said. "Don't make me go back."

The girl needed some reassurance and she gave her a hug.

"Never. You're safe. The man who helped you out is an undercover detective and I'm a bounty hunter. We're working this case together and anything you can tell us would help us save more girls. Do you know where they were taking you?"

She opened the car's back door and the girl sank down on the seat. Another girl rescued. One who didn't appear pregnant.

"This morning, they told me it was time to go. I was being moved to a new house."

"Did you have a baby?"

"No," the girl said perplexed. "Two days ago, walking home from a friend's house, they kidnapped me off the streets and locked me in a dark room."

The young woman's hands quivered. While she didn't appear hysterical, she almost seemed like after everything, she was going into shock.

"Look, this has been traumatic for you, but I really need you to tell me all you can so we can save other girls like yourself. Did you see any other young women?"

If she could give them some idea of the location of this house, that would be wonderful.

The girl shivered. "No, but music played until the wee hours of the morning. A loud booming beat. One night I woke to hear a girl crying. But I never saw anyone, but a man."

Could she identify Mateo? Katherine grabbed her phone and scrolled until she found the picture of him from their files.

"Do you recognize this man?"

The girl shuddered. "Yes, he's the one who kept telling me everything would be fine. That he rescued and would save me."

Another of Mateo's victims, but this girl they caught early. Worried the girl was having a reaction to the trauma she experienced, Katherine removed her coat and wrapped her jacket around her. "Don't go into shock on me now. Tell me everything from the beginning."

The girl shook her head. "My mother always told me not to walk the streets at night, but it was only two blocks, so I wasn't concerned. A white van stopped and two men jumped out."

The terror in her eyes gave Katherine chills.

"I tried to outrun them, but they grabbed me, and I fought, kicking and screaming until they put a white cloth over my nose and mouth. Later, I woke up in the dark room with a bathroom and a bed. Nothing else."

Haley shivered and wiped a tear from her eye. "That first night I was so scared and afraid they were going to rape me."

Reaching out, she patted her on the arm. "This is not easy, but you're doing a good job."

"The next day, that man came in and asked me all kinds of questions. Are you a virgin? Has a boy ever kissed you? At first, I refused to eat or drink anything, but eventually I was starving. I feared they would put some kind of drug in the food, so I ate very little."

As much as Katherine hated asking, she knew her responses would assist them know what they planned for this young woman. Where did they plan to take her?

"I'm not being personal, but I need the answers to those questions so I can determine why they asked. It will help us understand their plans for you, so we can save other trapped girls."

"Yes, I'm a virgin, one boy kissed me and no steady boyfriend, because I want to go to college."

"Good for you," Katherine said. "Your secrets are safe with me."

She didn't want to alarm the girl, but the police would require a physical exam and it was probably for the best. Just to make certain they hadn't given her drugs and or molested her. Still, this had to be terrifying for this young woman.

"This morning, they allowed me to shower and they gave me these clothes and told me time to go. That I was being transferred to the ranch."

"Ranch?"

"Yes, someplace where I would live forever, even though I kept saying I want to go home. They refused to let me go."

What were they going to do with her at a ranch? And how far from here?

"How many workers did you see?"

"Just the man you showed me and two other men, who when they looked at me, they scared me. The driver was one of the men who took me, and I think he's dead."

This was the first time they heard of the ranch. What did they do with the girls there?

Antonio was talking to the uniformed cops and the fire department. A car drove up and the case worker from the police had arrived.

"This is a lady from the police. She's going to call your parents and make certain you're all right. Always keep in mind you're one of the lucky girls. You got away before they had a chance to hurt you. If you remember anything at all, please contact me and the detective. One more thing," she said taking a deep breath.

"Don't let this ruin your life. Become the woman you dreamed of and put this behind you."

The girl teared up, she stood and threw her arms around Katherine. Her heart splintered, and she hugged the young woman back.

"Thank you, there is one thing I had forgotten."

"What? Any little thing can assist us."

"A cattle ranch. The driver said it would take almost an hour to arrive."

A helicopter hovered over the scene and Katherine tried to hide her face. Her cover would be blown if she showed up on the six o'clock news.

"That's perfect. That will help us locate the others. Anything else, please call me."

"Thank you, I will," the young girl said as the policewoman smiled at her.

"You ready to go home? Your mother is going to meet us at the hospital," she said.

"Yes, I want my family," she cried.

"Bye, Haley," Katherine said.

This never got easier and if she ever caught Mateo, his balls would be a prized possession. Yeah, she knew her thoughts were a little much, but when she thought of all the things he'd done, it gave her pleasure. The people he hurt. Enough. Time to catch him.

The policewoman led Haley away and Katherine hurried over to find Antonio. As much as she'd rather go home and crawl into bed with her case files, she needed to talk to him and tell him what she learned.

When she walked up, the forensics team was going through the man's pockets, looking for anything, but all he had on him was a burner phone. No driver's license, nothing. A veritable John Doe.

"Did you find anything on him?"

"Nothing," Antonio said. "Just him and the girl traveling down this road."

"Speaking of the girl, let's go for a stroll while the uniforms do their job," she said. Taking him by the arm, she led him away from the team Antonio had requested.

"The girl told me they were on their way to a ranch about an hour from here. A cattle ranch," she said. "She's not pregnant, they didn't touch her, in fact, she's a virgin. They told her she would love her life there. Could there be an illegal bordello operating somewhere near here?"

Staring at him, she didn't understand how she missed the information that Emma was his adopted daughter. The daughter of his heart and not of his loins. Could she have been talking about her biological dad and not Antonio.

That would make Katherine ten times the fool. And an even worse counselor. How had she not read this on her chart?

"Are you listening to me?" he asked.

"Sorry, my mind drifted off."

"Oh, you remembered that wonderful night of sex I gave you," he said, teasing her.

A blush rose to her face. "Concentrate. We need a map that shows all the ranches in this area approximately sixty minutes away."

"Give me some time and I'll have the station send us the maps on my computer," he said. "In the meantime, I think we've done everything we can here. The girl was taken to headquarters?"

Had Shaggy been trying to warn her Antonio was not at fault?

"Let me wrap things up with the officers and then we'll look to see what we have, and we'll go from there. Wait for me in the car."

Turning, he walked back to the overturned SUV that the tow truck was pulling onto its side. Why did everything feel like it was falling apart? If Antonio was Emma's adopted dad, she would have to apologize big time.

CHAPTER 30

*A*ntonio had the most incredible urge to pull the car over and kiss her senseless. Since they rescued Haley, Katherine had been quiet, almost too quiet. Sitting on the passenger side, her face was intense as she stared out the window.

"If we don't hurry, it will be dark before we arrive."

"This clunker is going as fast as it can."

"According to the map they sent us, there are three big farms and two smaller ones that fit the description of what Haley said. It's not perfect, but my gut says look at that one," she said, pointing to one of the smaller properties.

Why did she always argue with him and not just accept his word. A decorated police officer for almost fifteen years, the last five as a detective, he had some knowledge.

"And my gut is telling me go for the larger one. Think about it, they would have so much money, they could afford a bigger ranch. The cattle are decoys to make people think they're into farming."

He took a quick glance at her in the car as she studied the information. "I pulled up info on each of the owners. The smaller spread is owned by a group of individuals. Mateo did not have the money to start this himself. He needed backers."

"The reason why the larger farm seems more likely the one."

While he still thought she overreacted and was reckless, she was also extremely smart. Sometimes he believed she was smarter than him, but he would never admit that to her. He liked the way she researched everything she needed.

With a shake of her head, she said, "All right, we're going to each one to find out what we can. I'll flip to see whose ranch we go to first."

"Heads," he called.

"Darn it," she replied. "I always chose heads."

"Not this time. Flip the coin."

With a toss, it landed in her palm. When she opened her hand, the coin showed heads. "Damn."

"All right, we're headed to the Rockin' W ranch. Even the name sounds dirty."

Thirty minutes later, when they walked back to the car, she was laughing her ass off.

"How does your gut say now?"

"Like I've been betrayed," he said as they climbed back in. "For one thing, we were allowed to drive all the way to the main house. If they were running an illegal activity, they would stop us before we made it to the ranch home."

A twin-engine plane flew overhead coming in low as they watched him land beyond the horizon. "Who has their own landing strip around here?"

"Don't know," Antonio said. "See what you can find on the maps. Someone's flying in and out of here."

While he started the car and they drove up the roadway, Katherine searched the map. "Right here. A place called Little Piece of Paradise, owned by the Castano family."

"That kid that came to us at the station, his last name was Castano. Coincidence?"

Katherine cursed as she told him, "Doubtful. According to the property records, the land was purchased two years ago."

"Let's go," Antonio said and turned onto the highway. "Help me find the road that leads to the house."

The sun slowly slipped toward the horizon, and he knew it would be dark in fifteen minutes. Should they wait and come back another day and bring back up? But that voice inside his head refused to give up. They were so close.

As they turned down the drive, a rocky, deep rutted dirt road that had not been given much attention, he was tempted to turn back. There were rocks and ruts and yet it would make for an excellent way for them to realize someone approached.

Maybe this wasn't a good idea? Maybe they should wait for daylight, so they would know what they were getting into, and they could have a squad car accompany them.

Suddenly a bullet slammed into the car. Then another.

Katherine yanked out her Glock, unbuckled her seat belt just as the front window shattered. "Damn."

"Turn this heap around," she said and jumped into the back.

From the lowered back window, she returned fire. The police vehicle was being riddled with bullets. The sting of a bullet nicked him in the leg, and he knew they needed to go now or his daughter would soon be an orphan.

He spun the car around and picked up the radio. "Officer fired on. County road 1904," he said. "We're at Little Piece of Paradise ranch."

Katherine fired her Glock repeatedly, then she stopped and shoved another magazine in the gun. "Last magazine. Get us out of here now unless you want to be pushing up daisies."

A junk vehicle came racing toward them filled with men. "That's Mateo's car. We can't leave."

"Do you want to live," she asked.

What a silly question as he thought of the wound. The trickling of his blood down his leg overwhelmed him and for a

NAILING THE SINGLE DAD

moment, he feared he would pass out. The bullet tore through the tattered flesh of his left thigh, so his right foot at least could still operate the gas and brake.

"We've got to go now," she said, and he could hear her, but his concentration was becoming foggy. The image of Emma came to mind, and he pushed the car to its limits. The suspension would never be the same as it bounced on the rocky road toward the main road.

Once they hit the road, he gunned the gas. Glancing in the rearview mirror, no one followed them. As soon as the danger passed, his adrenaline slowed and, he began to feel dizzy. "You're going to have to drive."

"What?" she asked staring at him in the mirror.

"I'm passing out," he said. "And I can't stop the car."

The world went dark. A sudden stinging to his shoulder, jerked him awake.

"Don't you dare pass out on me. Pull over now," she screamed shaking him from the back.

"Did you just hit me?"

"You darn right I did," she said. "I'm not ready to die."

With the last of his strength, he pulled over just as a patrol car came alongside them.

"Detective Marino, is that you?"

"Yes," he said as Katherine jerked the door open and ran to his side. When she opened his driver's door, blood oozed down his leg forming a pool on the floorboard. The smell left him dizzy.

Helped to his feet, he wobbled as she clung to him.

"Where are you hurt? Where?" she demanded.

"My thigh," he groaned.

"Should I call an ambulance?" the uniformed officer asked.

"No time."

The man jumped out of his car to help.

"Hold him," she commanded.

Parked on the side of the road, she found duct tape in the

glove box and wrapped the tape tightly around his upper thigh, creating a tourniquet.

"Help me put him in the passenger side," she said to the policeman.

Woozy and swaying, they laid him in the back of the car.

"You lead the way, lights and sirens, and I'll follow you to the hospital."

"I'm not dying," he told her.

"No, you're not and we're going to make certain of that. Let's go."

CHAPTER 31

Damn him to hell. Yes, she was pissed. This day had not gone at all like she planned. Now she sat in the waiting room of the emergency room, sticking around for the doctor to decide whether they were going to keep Antonio or send him home.

And who was going to care for him at home? His daughter? Katherine couldn't volunteer because then they would both realize she was the daughter's counselor. That, she certainly didn't need or want. Especially after what she learned this afternoon. That he was the *adopted* father of Emma.

When she got back to the counseling office, she would check to see if the word adoption had been mentioned by either the parent or the child. But she didn't remember that information being on there. Why would he lie? Why would the daughter lie?

Was that data just a small fact she overlooked. No, she didn't think so, but still she needed to verify before she confronted them. Crap, the apology she owed him. All the rotten thoughts she said and how she told him she hated him.

"Come on back," the nurse said. "By the way, the tourniquet was a great idea. Saved him some pints of blood."

"Thank you, I was so scared."

Never before had she been so terrified he was seriously hurt. The realization that, if he died, she would have been devastated shook her. If he wasn't a baby daddy, her heart could be in serious trouble.

When she walked into the room, he appeared pale and tired. "Come here."

"What?" she asked as he pulled her into his arms, his mouth consuming hers. She didn't fight him, because she didn't want to. She liked the way his lips felt against her own, the way his mouth ravaged hers, the way her pulse raced inside her chest. A warmth began to flow through her body.

He ended the kiss, and she was not ready for them to stop. Oh, no, she wanted more. Leaning down, she covered his lips once again, the urge to climb in bed with him almost consuming her.

Someone cleared their throat and they broke apart. The doctor stood there, smiling.

"Mr. Marino, you are free to go home tonight. Keep the bandage clean. Set up an appointment with your regular doctor in about a week. In the meantime, you're off duty until your doctor clears you."

"Like hell," they both said at once.

A chuckle came from the man in the white coat. "Your leg is going to be weak. I won't fight you over going back to work, but I would suggest you take it easy.

"Sex will be painful the first few days. Good job on the tourniquet. Glad you weren't hurt any worse, Detective," he said as he walked out the door.

As soon as he was gone, she giggled. "Why did he think we were having sex?"

Though the idea spread warmth through her at the thought of the two of them.

"Maybe because you were deep throating me when he came in the door."

And she had been and loving every second.

"You started it."

"I was thanking you for getting me here safely and keeping the blood loss to a minimum."

"Well, that's good. So you don't want to kiss me anymore?"

He grabbed her arm and pulled her back to the bed. Once again, he kissed her like she'd never been kissed before. Any minute, she expected the Hallelujah chorus to come from the heavens above and for them to fall into bed and do it right there in the hospital.

Finally, she broke loose from him. "Have you called home and told them?"

Antonio frowned. "Look, if I go home with a bullet scrape down the side of my leg, my daughter is going to freak out. She's going to think that tonight she almost lost me."

It was true. Emma was beginning to recover from her mother's tragic death. Now for her father to have been shot, she would not take it well. Though he couldn't hide his wound from her forever. Sometime soon, he would need to tell her.

"Could I stay tonight at your place. Then tomorrow afternoon, I'll sit her down and tell her what happened. Explain its part of the job. We've talked about how I could be killed just like her mother. Emma knows the realities of working in law enforcement better than most kids."

Staring at him lying in the hospital bed, she wanted him to go home with her. Could he stay at her place without them yanking each other's clothes off and doing the nasty?

"No, there won't be sex tonight. I'm kind of dead from my waist down from the shot they gave me."

"Oh, wonderful, you want to spend the night with me and your dick isn't working," she said with a grin.

That was safer, because otherwise they would be in trouble.

And while she liked Antonio, a lot, was she ready to have sex with him?

A laugh rumbled from his chest. "You always know what to say. But yeah, I'm numb, not like you were that night I stayed with you before."

"That night is on the do not discuss list."

The lack of memories of what happened taught her one thing. The frightening peril of date rape drugs. Someday she would warn her girls about their dangers. Tonight might be nice to spend time with Antonio, just the two of them. Of course, being on pain pills he would be sleepy.

A grin spread across his face. "Well, tonight will also be on the do not discuss list, because I can't feel much down there at the moment."

"Who is staying with Emma?"

"Before you came in, I called Mrs. Langford. She's going to stay with her and I'm going to stay with you."

The nurse walked in and gave him his discharge papers, which he signed, and then they brought him a wheelchair to ride to the car.

"I'll get the poor damaged car and bring it around."

"Hurry back," he said. "I'd like to get in bed before the painkillers kick in."

CHAPTER 32

Once they arrived at her apartment, she managed to get him inside. From his expression, she could tell putting any weight on his leg was painful. What she had seen of bullet wounds, she never wanted to experience being shot. Just a scrape torn through his skin causing a small, but very deep laceration. One they glued together.

"Are you hungry?"

"No, but ice cream sounds good. Do you have ice cream?"

"Yes," she said with a smile. "Why don't we get you off that leg and I'll bring you a bowl."

He glanced toward her bedroom, and she shook her head and smiled. "Yes, you can sleep in my bed. No way, would I put you on the couch and my spare room is where my mother stays when she visits."

"You have a mother?"

"The smart-ass answers will get you kicked to the curb," she said, letting him lean on her as he limped into her room.

Last time, she woke up to him in her bed. This time, there were no illegal drugs rampaging through her system. This time, they were both very aware of each other as he sank down on the bed a grimace on his face.

"Sitting hurts worse than standing."

As she leaned down and took his shoes and socks off, she glanced at his pants. "On or off?"

"Hell, you've seen me naked before. Take them off, and leave my underwear on," he said, his voice breathless.

A smile crossed her face. "All I saw was your back and legs. You hid everything else from me."

"Your loss," he said, grimacing as he pulled his shirt out.

Reaching for his waist, she undid his belt, and he moved her hands away and snapped the button on his jeans and yanked the zipper down. His big green eyes, stared into hers, sending a tremor through her.

At the thought of waking beside him in the morning, a thrill spread from her chest.

Kneeling on the floor, she dragged his pants off very gently while he lifted himself off the bed. A scowl of pain crossed his face. The realization she hated seeing him hurting swept over her, and with a deep breath, she released the ache in her.

In her home, in her bedroom, the man filled the empty spaces. What was she doing with him here? Especially now that she realized the truth. That his daughter was adopted.

In fact, he was probably the most honorable man she had ever met. That frightened her, because even before she learned the truth, she knew she liked Antonio.

Chemistry existed between them that created fireworks.

She took his pants and laid them over a chair. Before she left the room, she helped him slide beneath the covers and propped pillows behind him. "Now for the ice cream."

"Aren't you going to put on your pajamas? We're having a sleepover kind of like the kids do."

Laughing, she went into her bathroom and dressed in her night clothes. The man would be severely disappointed if he thought they were sexy. Cotton top and bottoms with smiley faces all over them. One of her sorority sisters had given them to her as a gift.

Walking out, she stopped and modeled for him.

"Wow," he said. "No wonder you don't date. Those pj's would be a delight for men to rip from your body."

"Sarcasm equals less ice cream," she told him and hurried into the kitchen.

"Do you have chocolate?"

"No, vanilla, but I have sprinkles."

"Sprinkles? That's girly. Next sleepover is at my house and you're going to experience so many toppings."

"Next sleepover?" she said from the kitchen. "Are you planning on getting shot again?"

"Oh, hell no."

Katherine walked into the bedroom with two bowls of ice cream and handed him his before she crawled into the bed beside him.

"Vanilla. You need some spice in your life," he said, enjoying the spoonful of the creamy dessert. "I'm surprised you don't have cats."

Turning to face him, she raised her brows and gave him a look. "No time for any animals. I'm more of a dog person. There's a cat in the office. Merlin. Shaggy has Zeus, a rotten little dachshund, who you don't want to make mad. For some reason he likes to bite men in the balls."

"I think I'll avoid him."

For a moment, they ate their ice cream, and she wondered why the silence felt so easy. Like this was natural for the two of them to be sitting in bed, in pajamas, eating ice cream.

"Tell me about your family," he asked, and she turned to him astonished, wondering what brought that up.

This could be a way to ease into telling him she knew he wasn't a baby daddy. Was she ready to admit that to him, especially tonight when she was enjoying his company? What if he got mad and tried to leave?

No, not yet. Not until she understood what she wanted to say.

"My parents were divorced when I was ten and my sister eight. My father got my mother pregnant when they were young, and he married her, but always regretted not getting to live a free, wild, life. So when he reached his thirties, he decided he didn't want a family any longer and left us."

Taking another bite of ice cream, she remembered the day her relationship with her father came crashing down. Her twelfth birthday, she'd had enough. "For years, I tolerated him missing our weekends together until he missed my birthday. I told him don't come back. If he couldn't make time for me, I was done. Don't regret it one bit."

Antonio reached out and took her hand, his touch filled her with heat and his gaze seemed sincere. What was this man doing to her?

"No wonder you hate men and baby daddies."

But she didn't hate men. A lot of therapy helped her to see there were good available men. In her family, the women seemed to choose the losers. And she needed to be so careful as she gazed at the man rapidly claiming her heart.

"No, I don't dislike men, I just don't want anything to do with a man who could walk off and leave his children." The sweet cream was refreshing after thinking of her father.

"Why does it seem like in some families history repeats itself? When my sister was eighteen, she got pregnant by a guy who didn't want the responsibility of a family. I chased his ass down and made him pay child support until he legally gave up all claims to my nephew Grayson. And he had to get a vasectomy."

Antonio threw back his head and laughed. "What? Is that even legal?"

"Don't know. Don't care. Nicole was the second woman he'd

gotten pregnant and abandoned. Only this time, he messed with the wrong person, one who knew how to work the system. All done legally through a lawyer, but he was going to jail for past due child support. Either use birth control or keep your dick in your pants."

Yes, now it seemed cruel, but at the time she was going to college for her bachelors and had yet to receive the counseling she needed. Looking back, she was uncertain whether she had done the right thing.

The man couldn't support the children he had, and he was either unable or unwilling to keep his penis locked down. After two unwanted babies, you would think he would learn. Maybe he was searching for the perfect love or some other bullshit.

When finished with their ice cream, she glanced at Antonio and took the empty bowl from him.

"Remind me to never piss you off," he said, staring at her in amazement.

"All done, through proper legal channels. We would drop the charges if he gave up rights to Grayson and if he received a vasectomy."

After setting their dishes on the nightstand, she scooted down in the bed.

"How did your sister handle your interfering? And your mother?"

A chuckle came from her. "They were so relieved he was out of their lives. Now Nicole has been accepted into college and is going to start working part-time with the agency."

After everything Nicole had been through, she was really proud of the way her sister changed her life. Grayson, her nephew was so adorable.

Scooting down beside her, he pulled out the extra pillows and rolled over on his good leg and stared at her. "Now I understand you. But I want you to know, I would never leave a woman who had my child. What a gift—a son or daughter of you own."

What could she say that would not end this night on a sour note? If she admitted to him she made a mistake, he would want to know why she believed that now. Tomorrow, she needed to verify the paperwork. Someday she would tell him, but not tonight. Not now.

"Since we're having a slumber party. Tell me about your wife."

"Damn you know how to ruin a party," he said with a sigh. "What can I say? I loved her dearly. Sheila was working late night patrol, which is always the most dangerous. That afternoon, when I came home, she kissed me goodbye and said she would see me in the morning. That was the last time I spoke to her."

Tears filled his eyes. "About four that morning, her commanding officer called me and told me to get to the hospital. To take Emma. Right after we arrived, she took her last breath. In a deep unconscious state, she waited for us to say goodbye before she let go."

"That must have been hard." Katherine could not imagine being awakened with that kind of call. The fear and hope and prayers and then abruptly it ends and not the way you want.

"The hardest part was all the publicity. Dallas cop killed in the line of duty. The endless parade of people coming to your house. The press, the funeral, and her clothes hanging in the closet. Like any moment she would return."

She reached out and touched his hand, squeezing it and running her fingers up and down his arm, trying to release the tension she could feel there. Now she understood Emma's pain even better. Now she understood Antonio's loss.

"Suddenly everything is over and you have to learn to live without her. Suddenly I became both mother and father. The two of you must find out how to live with a hole in your family."

With a sigh, he pushed her hair away from her face.

"Enough. We're doing fine. Three years have passed and now I dodge friends who want to set me up with a really lovely woman. When you arrive, she's beautiful, but she hates kids, would insist I quit the force and no, she would never live in another woman's home."

With a laugh, he stared at her. "After three blind dates, now I'm always busy."

"So you're not dating?"

"No, too much drama."

"Agreed," she said and rolled toward him. They were almost head-to-head facing one another, staring into one another's eyes. Katherine had never experienced anything like this before. She'd never been so close to another human being like this.

Tilting his head, his face leaned in next to hers. "Damn, but I need to kiss you."

She had been lying here beside him needing him to at least kiss her. His mouth covered hers, and she sighed as his lips consumed her own. His tongue swept the inside of her mouth as her hands reached up and held his mouth in place while he ravished her lips.

With a sigh, they broke apart, and she gazed into his eyes and could see the painkillers starting to work.

"As much as I enjoyed that, I think it's time for lights out," she said.

A groan came from him. "Damn drugs they gave me. I'm still numb, or we would be doing so much more."

"Maybe it's better this way."

"Only if you'll hold me until I fall asleep."

"That I can do," she promised. "That I can do."

CHAPTER 33

The next morning, lying in bed beside her, Antonio wanted one thing and only one thing. Katherine. Even though his leg was sore, there was one area of his body that refused to stop thinking of this woman.

Him curled around her, she snuggled up against him, pushing her buttocks into his pelvic region. Though she'd been asleep, she suddenly tensed.

"Antonio," she said softly.

With his mouth, he nuzzled her neck. "No more numbness."

"I noticed."

Turning around, she faced him. "But your leg."

There were other parts of him that were hurting worse than his thigh.

"To hell with the leg. It's going to hurt regardless," he said, kissing along her shoulders feeling the ripple of her skin.

"We shouldn't," she said, raising her chin to give him better access to her throat.

Sometimes, even when comprehending you were treading in dangerous territory, you went ahead and took a chance. And Antonio wanted this opportunity with Katherine.

NAILING THE SINGLE DAD

"Probably, but this morning before the world intrudes, I'd like to spend some time with you. Finishing what we've danced around now for a week."

With a shove of his hand, he pushed up her pajama top and searched for her nipple.

Layering his mouth around the nub, he sucked the orb between his lips. Why was he so attracted to this woman when he pledged to himself he would never marry again after Sheila, but he couldn't resist her.

"Unless you want me to stop."

"You stop and you won't have to worry about another bullet," she promised.

A chuckle escaped from his chest. "I'm taking that for a yes."

"Dear God, yes."

With a groan, he pulled her mouth to his, melding with her as she opened to his onslaught of passion.

Oh, God, he felt like this was where he belonged.

Running his hand beneath her pajamas, his fingertips skimmed her smooth leg until he found the edge of her panties and slipped his fingers under the scrap of lace.

She broke the kiss and pushed away from him, her eyes wild, her breathing quick as she stared at him. "We're playing with fire."

"A fire only we can extinguish," he said as his lips covered hers once again. Now was not the time to listen to reason, excuses, or any logical talk. Not now. Not when he needed her so badly.

Her hands held his mouth to hers, and desire rattled him as he pressed his body against her, his erection nestled next to her belly.

Yes, he shouldn't want her so desperately. Yes, he shouldn't crave her like he wanted his next breath. But he did, and she was here, his for the taking.

Longing for Katherine had been building since they started working together. Since the first day he met her, he'd been drawn to her except for her smart tongue that lashed him for something he would never do. Now, she seemed to accept him.

Pushing away, she took a deep breath. "Wouldn't this be easier without my pajamas."

"I thought you'd never agree. And my bad leg is not going to let me remove them from you," he said, his breathing harsh. The very idea of seeing her naked again sent his pulse racing.

Jumping out of bed, she quickly removed her pajama bottoms and top while he struggled to expel his nightshirt and underwear.

Naked, she came to his rescue and leaned over him and pulled his boxers down past his penis, which jumped to attention.

"Looks to be working just fine," she said with a grin, her breasts hanging over him.

Staring at her, he thought she was more beautiful than he remembered from the last time with her shapely hips and long legs. There was no turning back. Breathing was next to impossible as he stared at her firm breasts and narrow waist.

"Thank goodness," he said, and lowered his mouth back to her. Like he suffered from a long drought of kisses, he kissed her like he'd forgotten the feel of lips beneath his. The way a woman softly moaned deep in her throat. The way she made him feel manly and strong.

Teasing, he slid his hand down the back of her head, her neck, to her breasts where he tweaked her nipple. A groan escaped from her.

Right now, he only wanted Katherine surrounding him as he surged within her. His fingers found her center, and he let them do all the talking in a language only lovers knew. One where they both rode a rocket, orbited the moon, and returned to earth totally shattered. One where, this time, he would join Katherine on that voyage.

He knew his strength wouldn't last long. Light as a feather,

her fingertips skimmed over the solid muscles of his chest and abdomen, sending his pulse racing through him. A hissed rush of breath escaped him and a soft satisfied smile crossed her face.

This morning would be theirs to last them for the rest of their lives. This morning, they would quench this fire between them, and when the investigation was over, go their separate ways.

Because Antonio would never let another person receive that devastating phone call that ripped your heart out. As long as he was in law enforcement, there would be no wife, no lover, no one to be hurt like he experienced.

His erection sprang at her, hard and rigid and eager. She wrapped her fingers around his penis, fisting him as she stroked him.

Desire flooded through him like a spring thunderstorm.

When his tongue swept across her breast, she arched her back in a fevered response. Heat blazed throughout him, leaving him needy.

Urgent to touch her, eager to skim her satin skin, he reached out and ran his fingertips down her face in a loving caress. Though they fought each other at every turn, they'd always been good together.

"Condom," he gasped

"No, I don't have any," she said, sagging to the bed.

"My pants. Inside my billfold," he said. It was an old one he had carried for many years and should have been replaced.

Jumping out of bed, she ran to his pants and found the foil packet in his wallet.

"Thank God," she said and hurried back.

Ripping the condom package open, he quickly sheathed himself.

"You're going to have to do most of the work," he moaned, and she did.

Climbing on top of him, careful to avoid his leg, she

welcomed him as he slid within the confines of her body, capturing him inside her, holding him tightly. A deep sigh of satisfaction released through him as he stared up into her beautiful brown eyes.

Gripping her hips, he slowed the urgency, knowing he would be done in no time and wanting to give her the satisfaction they both deserved. As he realized the impact of what they were doing, he paused, and then he slowly eased almost all the way out, before plunging her down once again.

Swiftly, his need rose, and he opened his eyes and stared deeply into hers, wanting to touch her soul and brand her as his own.

Unhurried, he took her mouth, his lips consuming hers. He wanted to consume her as desire rippled through her like an aftershock. Their tongues mated and danced as his lips moved over hers. Why with this woman did he experience so much passion? Why did his body respond like he had come home?

"Antonio," she said, her voice shaky and needy.

With each thrust, Katherine rode him, her hips moving of their own accord, her body completely in tune with his. They moved as one, in unison, in perfect harmony.

Their lips broke apart and she gasped. "Don't stop."

With a smile, he pounded into her again and again and again. Unimaginable pleasure spiraled through him, leaving him breathless and dizzy.

Magic filled him, tightening, centering and sizzling with an intensity that stunned him. With only one other person had he ever experienced such satisfaction.

Her brown eyes darkened as her body shuddered release. Antonio let go of the orgasm he felt gathering like a storm inside his body. Tremors rippled through him. Clasping her back, he held her tightly, wanting to absorb her into his soul, where he could cherish these moments together. He was hers.

Avoiding his leg, she slumped on top of him before she rolled to his side. For a moment, the two of them lay there as their breathing returned to normal and their heartbeats slowed.

The room was silent except for the sound of their lungs spasming for more air. Reality crashed in like a two-ton rock; the condom had broken.

CHAPTER 34

Two days later, Katherine could not get Antonio out of her head. The morning they spent together in her bed had lasted into the afternoon, when he finally said he needed to get home and visit his daughter.

They had laughed, made love, and when she took him home, she feared what came next. Especially since she knew once she confirmed his daughter's notes, she would owe him an apology. One he was not going to be happy receiving when he learned she was his Emma's counselor.

How had they gotten to this point?

Today was the day she met with the girls for their weekly counseling session. She arrived an hour early to go through her notes and see what Emma's file said. As she sat down to read the report, she groaned. Nowhere in the files was it noted Antonio was her adopted father.

Her mentor, Pat Brindle came through the door. "Ready for today?"

"Did you know Emma's father, Detective Antonio Marino, is not her biological father?"

Hope spiraled through Katherine. Maybe she wasn't a bad counselor.

"No, I didn't. There was a huge uproar when her mother was killed three years ago as a police officer on duty, but why isn't Emma with her birth father?"

Now, Katherine wanted to go back through all her notes to see what Emma said that made her believe Antonio was her baby daddy.

"When Antonio married her mother, he adopted Emma. The father she dislikes and talks so badly about in session is her birth father. Not Antonio."

The woman frowned. "That should have been in the records somewhere. Why didn't we have this information before and how did you find out?"

There were too many hidden facts or lying going on. From here on out, Katherine needed to be different. She had to learn to control her potty mouth and not jump to assumptions before she passed judgement.

"Antonio and I are investigating a case that involves sex trafficking and adoption black markets. We've been working together and I thought the absolute worst of him. Until he told me he adopted his daughter."

All this time, she had believed him to be the scum of the earth when in fact he was a good guy. One of the best, and she just hoped this didn't ruin whatever kind of relationship they were trying to establish.

The woman took a chair and sat across from Katherine. "Though you want to tell him, you cannot violate the Hippa laws by talking to him about the sessions. That would be violating the child's trust. Even if he's her father, the only way we can say anything to him is if there is a problem we feel needs discussing."

Apologizing was going to be so tricky. How do she say *I'm*

sorry I assumed the worst about you from what was said in your daughter's counseling sessions?

"Understood and I've not said a word to him. He's the one who told me his daughter was adopted and I about fell out of my chair. All this time, I had such horrible thoughts of him and now I realize he's innocent."

The woman nodded. "In this business, you must learn not to accept everything people say in a session. There are always two sides to a story. If possible, find out both sides before passing judgement."

Katherine sighed. Of course, she still wanted to be a counselor and help these young girls, but she needed to be more objective. It was so easy to become involved in their stories and she immediately went to battle for them.

"Very sound advice that I see the wisdom in taking. It's been a busy few days. For today's session, I want to make Emma clarify to everyone her real father is the abuser. Honestly, I don't think she thinks of her birth father as important any longer."

"Agreed, but still, she should have clarified to all of us," Pat said.

While she enjoyed leading these sessions, the counselor had been very clear that she had some issues of her own. Said her behavior was a result of the pain and hurt she felt with her father leaving. Which made her relate to the girls.

"Are you going to continue in counseling? I know you were considering dropping the classes."

Katherine smiled at her. "Every time I think I'm going to quit and stick with bounty hunting, we experience a breakthrough. Someone learns something that leaves them better. Including me. My heritage draws me to our agency and yet my heart wants me here. I'm still not certain I can give up Lipstick and Lead."

Now torn between her chosen profession and her heritage, especially with the announcement of Jennifer's pregnancy, what would she choose? The agency would be short of bounty hunters for a while, but she did love working with young girls to help them become stronger.

"There's still time," Pat said. "My report at the end of the semester will show how you have grown and changed as a person. With your experience, you relate to these preteen young ladies and you'll be a wonderful counselor in the field."

All this time, she didn't believe Pat liked her, but here she was recommending her and that thrilled Katherine. "Thank you."

"I'm proud of the work you've accomplished. Now come on, we better get going, the session is about to start."

Together, they walked out of the office into the room where they held the sessions. The girls came in and sat talking amongst themselves as Katherine waited for everyone to arrive.

When the last girl came running in, Katherine closed the door. "Hi, ladies."

"Hi," they responded.

"We've got a lot to cover this afternoon, so let's start with everyone telling us how you're doing."

As they went around the circle, each one told how they were feeling. Later, she would learn what really troubled them. Usually something would come out when they were talking.

"Emma, I have a question for you," she said. "Who is your real father?"

"My birth father is Brian Hall, but my father is Detective Antonio Marino," she said.

Before Katherine could ask her if she had told any of them this before, the door slammed open, and they all jumped. Standing in the doorway stood Mateo.

Fear almost paralyzed her as her heart skipped a beat.

"What the hell," she said, thinking her Glock was in her purse in the office. Too far for her to reach it. "What do you want?"

"Gorgeous," he said, walking into the room. "What a coincidence. Bounty hunter who works with the detective and now a counselor. You're a busy lady. And look at all these girls."

Air rushed from her lungs as fear consumed her.

Did Mateo hear Emma tell who her father was? Please, God, she prayed he hadn't heard anything. The door closed shut behind him.

"You've got my girl," he said. "Her mother and I don't want her here any longer."

He stepped close to Katherine who was doing her best to remain calm in front of the girls. Leaning into her, he grinned. "Beautiful, you know what's going to happen to her."

A chill rippled through Katherine, and she gazed at Ashley who had slipped behind one of the couches. "She's not here. Ashley skipped today."

He gazed around the room and stopped when he saw Emma. "Oh, she's here. The little coward is hiding behind the couch."

"Is her mother with you?"

Per the law, they were not to leave without one of their parents with them.

"No," he said grinning. "She's had a little accident."

Oh, no. What had he done to Ashley's mother?

"Per state law, you can't take her."

"Who's going to stop me? You, bounty hunter?" In a flash, he pulled out his gun and waved the weapon around the room. The girls all screamed and ducked. "No, I'm taking her and Detective Marino's daughter."

Emma gasped.

How could she prevent him from taking them? Somehow she had to keep him from stealing these young women. Antonio would hate her forever if he took Emma.

"No," Katherine begged. "Take me instead. I'll go with you."

A booming laugh came from him, and he pushed her back with his gun. "And have to put up with your nonsense, no. These girls are trainable. You're not. These beautiful ladies will fetch a high dollar on the market."

"No," Katherine screamed. "No, you can't take them. No."

Reaching out, he grabbed Emma and approached Ashley who still hid behind a couch. "Come on, you little tramps. You belong to me now."

Shoving the girls toward the door, he waved the gun around, and he pointed his automatic weapon at Katherine. "Follow me and they die. Now pick up the phone and call the detective and tell him I'm done playing his cat and mouse game. Game over and I win. Look at my prize."

Of course, he would. Antonio would go after Emma and Mateo knew it.

"If you think you'll get away with this, you're crazy. He'll bring the cavalry to rescue his daughter and Ashley."

"Oh, I'm hoping he will come charging after her, so I can kill him."

Fear spiraled through Katherine at the thought of Antonio being killed. The man's honor would require he give himself up to save Emma and that frightened her even more.

The door slammed after him and Katherine raced out into the hall hoping to stop him. Turning, he fired his weapon, and she had to duck to keep from getting shot.

"Back off or the next bullet goes into Emma's brain."

Taking the stairs two at a time, she hurried up to the office where she left her gun and her phone.

Quickly she dialed Antonio as she walked out the door.

"They have Emma," she cried.

CHAPTER 35

*A*ntonio was lying on the couch, looking at his notes on his iPad about the investigation. Why did he feel like they had missed some small detail that would break this thing wide open? Something they'd overlooked.

This case started out as an investigation of a man drawing TANF welfare for five women. He'd also skipped his bail hearing and was wanted for molestation of a minor. But this turned into so much more with rumors of sex trafficking and most definitely the black-market adoption agency.

There had to be more to this operation than one man. Could the FBI not be connecting the dots and another investigation connected with this one?

While reading, his phone rang. "Hello, beautiful."

"Antonio, Emma and Ashley were taken this afternoon," Katherine said, her voice tight and full of fear.

"What are you talking about? She's at her counseling session," he said, laying the iPad aside, sitting up and starting to put his shoes on. Whatever was happening, Katherine sounded distraught.

"Mateo barged into the room. Emma had just said something

about you being her father, and he must have overheard her. He recognized me immediately, and then he took the two girls."

"What the hell were you doing in her counseling session."

A long pause and finally she said, "I'm the intern who is running the group. For the last four months, Emma has been a client."

A fierce rush of anger went through him. "All this time you said nothing."

"I couldn't. Even now I'm breaking the Hippa law."

"But I'm her father. I should know who is counseling her."

"And Mrs. Pat Brindle is the counselor, but as her intern, I've been sitting in. We've got to find Emma and Ashley. Mateo said he would kill her if the police show up. He wants you to come after her, and he will murder you and keep Emma. Don't leave. I'm on my way."

Terror gripped him at the thought of his beautiful daughter as he disconnected the phone and started to gather his tactical gear. What he wore in a hostage situation, only this time it was Emma that was kidnapped. Damn Mateo, he would kill him with his bare hands if he touched his daughter.

CHAPTER 36

*A*s Katherine drove to pick up Antonio, her brain scrambling to find an answer to where he would take the girls. With a slap to the head, she realized one person might be able to help her.

"Call contact," she said as she drove like a crazy woman through the streets of Dallas.

"RESPONSE."

"Shaggy," she said and the car dialed his number. Thank God for automatic phones.

"What's up?"

"Emma Marino and Ashley were kidnapped by Mateo."

The man cursed.

"He broke into the session and stole them right out from under me. There was no way for me to stop him. I didn't have my gun and..." A sob escaped from her. Now was not the time to lose it. She was driving and she needed information.

"Take a deep breath," Shaggy said. "I'll call my informants and see what I can learn."

With a quick gulp, she said, "Are there any whorehouses or places men go for sex in the downtown Dallas area near the

Pegasus? One girl told me she could see the flying red horse from the window in her room."

For a moment Shaggy was silent, and she feared she'd lost her connection until he groaned. "Located on Commerce Street is a very exclusive gentleman's club for the wealthy. No signs, nothing that would let you know it's a brothel or even an entertainment venue. To join the club, you pay big money to receive the code."

She would bust down every door to the place if she had too to find these girls. They had been taken from her and even though Antonio was going with her, his injured leg would slow him down. Mateo would kill him on sight and probably her as well, but she had to try.

"Oh, I'll have no problem getting in. What's the address?"

"Be careful. A wealthy family owns the building. The Castanos."

"Son of a bitch, someone named Tomas Castano came into the police office and spoke to Antonio. Said his girlfriend was missing."

"The Castanos are a rich, powerful Dallas connection and their girls are hand selected."

"Including underage girls?"

Shaggy sighed. "Can't answer that, but the security is tight. Are you on your way?"

"No, I've got to pick up Antonio. Then we'll head that direction. Text me the address."

"Get a search warrant. I'll meet you there," he said.

"No, I don't want you to blow your cover and Mateo will kill the girls if we come with anyone else."

Silence filled the airwaves on the phone. "Katherine, you scare me. Often times you leap before you look. Be careful. That club is known as a dangerous place. Antonio is going to be with you?"

"Yes," she said, but he didn't know the detective had been

shot. Why did everyone believe she wasn't cautious? "Gotta go, I'm in front of Antonio's house."

The man came hurrying out prepared for combat duty.

"Shaggy just gave me a tip on where they might be. But I need you to obtain a search warrant," she said.

When he got in the car, his limp barely noticeable, his body stiff, his eyes flashing daggers, Antonio didn't say a word. Oh, yeah, he was furious.

"Where," he said.

"You remember that girl who told us she saw the Pegasus from her window. Shaggy gave me the name of a club that operates downtown. No names, no signs, nothing, but a building you must have the password for the door to open. The Castano family owns the whorehouse."

Antonio glared at her. "Son of a bitch. If I find that little creep, he'll spend extra time in jail for lying to us."

Just then her phone dinged with the address Shaggy had texted. Antonio grabbed the cell and glanced at it, his face frowning.

"I know this address. We busted someone here two years ago," he said.

"Did Mateo call?"

"Nothing."

That was frightening because what if he killed the two girls?

He pulled out his phone. "Chad, Mateo has captured my daughter and another girl. Yes, but I don't care. We're going into a gentleman's club on Commerce Street. What can you tell me about this building that is owned by the Castano family? I need a search warrant."

The FBI agent was talking and from Antonio's body language, he was growing more agitated by the minute.

"Uh huh. How much money did they pay the FBI to keep quiet? Do you think I give a rat's ass who owns the building, the business or anything else? My daughter could be there and I'm going to find her.

"Get me a search warrant," he yelled at the agent.

Enraged, she had never seen him so angry. If possible, he would have thrown the phone.

"What?"

"That suited dick knew exactly which building. A club where you can have any pleasure you want and is run by one of the highest profile criminals in the state."

"The FBI had information all along about this place?"

"Yes. He said they checked it out and gave them the all clear. Then he warned me about going into the club. The FBI didn't want any bad publicity. Screw him.

"I don't give a fuck about their publicity problem." Antonio's face turned beet red as he gritted his teeth. "We're going in with or without them."

Katherine pulled the car up in front of the address and put it in park. Yes, she was blocking a lane of traffic, but they would have to deal with it. They had two girls to rescue.

CHAPTER 37

Antonio was furious. No one messed with his daughter. No one stole her from a safe place right before her counselor's eyes without dealing with him. No one lied to him about his daughter. And yet Katherine had.

No wonder she believed he was a baby daddy. Emma went to the counseling sessions to overcome the fact that not only had her birth father not wanted her, but her mother died.

Katherine must have thought he was Emma's birth father. On any legal paperwork, he was listed simply as her father. Nothing about Emma being adopted. After all, she was his child. Not the sperm donor who walked away.

Now she'd been abducted. Damn Katherine for not keeping her safe.

As they hurried to the door, he noted cameras were everywhere. "Dallas police, open up," he demanded.

While the doors looked like no one could enter, he would force his way in if they didn't open. "We have a search warrant."

She gazed at him, her brows drawing together, questioning. At the last second, Chad had come through for him, and yes, indeed he had a search warrant.

"On the count of three, I'm busting down this door."

Still, no response. Taking out his Glock he motioned for Katherine to stay behind him as he shot the lock off the door. They pushed through and rushed inside where half-naked women were running. Reaching out, he grabbed one by the arm and stopped her. "Where is Mateo?"

The woman shrugged and kept on moving.

Raising his gun, he fired a shot in the air and everyone froze. "That's better. I'm looking for Mateo and two young girls. Anyone who has seen them gets a free get out of jail card. The rest of you are going downtown."

"Downstairs," one of the ladies yelled. "Hurry he is about to leave."

A pulsing beat pounded through the building, off to the side, a room where ladies must dance for prospective gentlemen. The temptation to light a match and watch this place burn overwhelmed him, but that would endanger innocent lives. Women who hadn't come here of their own accord.

The owner would definitely be spending time behind bars for this outfit.

Pushing their way through the scantily clothed women standing around staring at them a glazed look in their eyes, he realized they must've been drugged.

Rushing downstairs, because of his sore leg, Katherine was in front, her Glock out and ready to fire. Down here, the rooms were dark, cold and the sound of crying coming from one somewhere.

Not bothering to plan their attack, Katherine started opening the doors. In her belt, she carried a small hammer and at a locked door, she busted it open, freeing the young girl inside. This must be the training area. The place where they kept the newbies. Each room held a young underage girl.

"Up the stairs and wait outside. The police are up there, and they will protect you."

"Emma?"

Knowing it was probably not the smartest of things to do, but he couldn't hold back any longer to learn if she was down here or not.

One of the girls shouted. "They took her out the back. Hurry."

Damn his leg for being such a stiff pain, but he hurried around a corner. Katherine ran in front of him, and he wanted to grab her and pull her back to safety. No telling what they would find when they reached the back area.

"Wait, Katherine. You're going off all cockeyed."

In typical Katherine style, she ignored him and raced ahead. Why wouldn't this stubborn woman slow down instead of running toward danger.

As she rounded a back wall, she raised her Glock and shouted. "Let her go. Now."

Katherine fired her weapon as he came around the corner to see Mateo trying to force a struggling Emma into a car. The back alley smelled of garbage and rats and other vile smells. And his daughter fought the jerk as she tried to be brave while the adults around her lost their minds.

The gutless bastard put the gun to Emma's head and Antonio felt his heart stop. Mateo's eyes were wild with fright. "Back off or she's dead."

"She's dead if she gets in that car," Katherine shouted. "Drop your weapon. Now."

The man stood, watching as she approached. Damn the woman was going to get herself and Emma killed.

Suddenly he saw a man from the Lipstick and Lead Agency on the other side of the car approaching. What was he doing here? He gave Katherine the address.

Antonio attempted to sneak up on the opposite side, hoping to leap out and surprise Mateo. Still, that gun was held to his daughter's head.

"Mateo, let the girl go and I'll go with you," she said. "Let them go and I'll go with you."

"We've already discussed this, and I said no. This is a trick."

What was Katherine doing? Trading herself for the girls. No, he would never let that happen. Just no.

"No, it's not. If you take those girls, you're going to die. Take me and you have a good chance of getting out of here."

Shaggy slipped closer behind them and Antonio tried to lined up a direct shot at Mateo, but a concrete pillar stood in the way.

"I'll even put down my weapon to show you good faith."

What the hell was she doing? Now he could kill her with one bullet. In disbelief, he observed her set her Glock on the ground.

Mateo started laughing. "What's to stop me from taking you and my lovely angels. I'm a selfish bastard who wants it all."

While Mateo was talking, Katherine inched closer and closer to the man. Heart in his throat, Antonio watched as she sprang at Mateo, knocking him away from Emma. Struggling with him over the gun.

Shaggy rushed around the corner to pull Emma and Ashley to safety.

Fear exploded inside Antonio at the realization either one of them could die at any second.

A loud blast filled the alley outside the building as Mateo fired, hitting Katherine in the upper right chest just as she knocked his weapon out of his hand. Like a rag doll, she collapsed to the ground and didn't move.

Pain detonated inside Antonio as he realized she had been shot.

"No," Antonio cried as Mateo scrambled for the loose gun. Quickly he pulled the trigger, firing off two shots hitting him in the leg and also the foot. The man screamed in agony.

The Dallas police came running down the back alley. Mateo lay on the ground screaming and cursing obscenities. Antonio yanked him up and slapped the wrist ties on him, not caring if he hurt his wounds.

"He's all yours."

Shaggy, Emma, and Ashley raced to Katherine. She had to be dead. The chances of surviving that kind of shot close up...

"We've called an ambulance," Emma said, holding her hand.

Shaggy shook his head. "You are one stubborn woman."

Oh, how he wanted to go to her, but tears rolled down his cheeks. If she was dying, he couldn't take another loss. Not after the last one. To lose another woman he loved to violence would gut him.

Gathering his courage, he limped to Katherine's side and knelt beside her.

"Damn it. I told you to wait," he said, his tears flowing unheeded. Not again.

"Patience is not my virtue," she said weakly. "Hurts like a mother..."

He knew what she wanted to say, but with Emma there, kept her language clean.

"Why did you do that? If you'd just waited."

"For what? Them to kill Emma and Ashley? You? Like that was going to happen. He's captured. The girls are safe. Now I think I want to go to sleep."

"No," he said as her eyes slowly closed. "Stay with me. Don't leave."

The paramedics had arrived, and they moved them out of the area as they loaded her onto a gurney.

All he could do was pray she wasn't dead.

CHAPTER 38

Antonio had one of the patrol officers drop Emma off at home where Mrs. Lancaster promised to be waiting. She wanted to go to the hospital, but he didn't think that was such a good idea. Emma needed normalcy and routine.

Katherine and he had driven over the cliff. He would be here by her side until he was certain she would make it, then he would break away. An impulsive, risky person who would one day meet a bullet with her name on it, bringing her to an end.

And he couldn't be there to see her die.

Yes, he loved her. Last night, when she risked everything, he realized he loved her and would never go through losing another wife. It ripped his soul out and kicked it to the curb.

The days of staring into space and wondering how this could happen to his family. The days of waking up thinking he heard her coming in the door from her shift.

Watching his child suffer wanting her mother and learning the hard reality that she would never be back. No, he couldn't do it again.

When he reached the waiting room, the whole family was there. Her cousins, Jennifer and Carson, Brittany and Mark,

Gina, Uncle Sam, Shaggy, her mother and sister. Even Chad, the FBI detective, Kevin Harris and Pat Brindle. They all started clapping when he walked in the door.

"Congratulations," his boss said, coming up to him, "the two of you broke up the largest prostitution, sex trafficking ring in Texas and also a subsequent black-market adoption agency.

"Seems once the girls became pregnant, they sold the babies. The two of you did an outstanding job. Now the department will be reuniting these young women with their families."

Thinking of Emma, he shook his head. "This case gave me nightmares. The worst investigation I've ever worked on. Thank you. How's Katherine?"

Her mother walked up to him and gave him a slant eye. "Are you the man who has been working with Katherine?"

"Yes, ma'am. How is she?" Why wouldn't someone tell him how she was doing? Was it so serious she was dying? What?

The woman threw her arms around him. "Since she's been involved with you, we've seen such a difference in her attitude. You calm her."

That was interesting. During the last few weeks, she became a different person, but she still had a careless cocky demeanor that would someday get her killed. "Please, how is she? Can I see her?"

"She's in surgery," her mother said. "The doctor came out and said she's doing better, but she's not out of the woods."

"Thank you," he said and walked over to the seat he sat in while he waited in this same room to learn if Jennifer would survive.

Why did these bounty hunter women seem prone to gun shots? You would think they would want to find another profession. One where they hurried home to their family instead of chasing bad guys.

Uncle Sam and Gina strolled to his side. Gina had her hand laid on the old man's arm in a possessive way that clearly let everyone know she and the uncle were an item.

"Oh, honey, we're so proud of the two of you and how you saved those young girls," Gina said. "You and Katherine make such a great team."

What could he say? The woman was trying to push him and her together, and he could not accept her reckless, dangerous, crazy ways. Sooner or later, somebody would get killed with her around. Or she would be the one taking a bullet that ended it all.

"Thank you," he said, feeling inadequate. With Katherine's help, he'd done his job. Saved his daughter and kept his life from totally falling apart.

Jennifer and Brittany walked over to him. Jennifer smiled. "Congratulations on the big case. We're so glad you two stopped these criminals. Um, I wondered about the two of you."

The look he gave her clearly said don't ask, but she did. "Are you two an item now? I mean, you sent her flowers the last time she was in the hospital."

Now he understood why Emma sent flowers. Because Katherine was her counselor and also she wanted the two of them together. For the longest, he didn't understand why, but now it all came clear to him. "No."

"Oh," Brittany said. "I thought you stayed over at her house a couple of times."

"We were working. That's all," he said, thinking somehow he needed to end this with Katherine and soon. Before her family started making long term plans. Before everyone believed because they worked together, they were dating.

His chest ached at losing what they had just begun and not seeing her again. But it was necessary. For his and Emma's sake, this must end.

After they wandered off whispering, Pat, the woman who led the sessions his daughter attended came to his side.

"I'm sure you're angry at Katherine."

His jaw dropped, anyone could see his emotions. He jerked his head and looked at her. "Yes."

"When she told me she knew you, I told her we should disclose to you she was sitting in your daughter's sessions. But she didn't want to embarrass either of you. So we kept silent.

"This afternoon, she arrived at the office early to check out Emma's paperwork. There was nothing about adoption on the papers. These girls have helped Katherine, and she's been good for them."

In the scheme of things, that no longer seemed very important. Sure, he wished she would have told him, trusted him, but after tonight, he only wanted her to survive. Then he could end things with her before she got herself killed.

Just then the doctor came in, and they all stopped talking.

"Katherine is doing well. We removed the bullet. She lost a lot of blood, so we're giving her more now, but she should be in recovery in the next hour."

Relief surged through him, followed closely by dread. Tonight, he would peek in and say hello. Once they had everything wrapped up with the case, he would end the relationship. He needed to.

CHAPTER 39

Katherine hated lying in a hospital bed with absolutely nothing to do. Bored, she was ready to return to her sessions with the girls. Pat, her supervisor had come by, and they made the decision from now on when it came time to meet, the door would be locked.

Unbeknownst to Pat, she also determined, she would hide a small pistol in her pants pocket.

Hopefully, she would never need it again, but for the two young girls to go through so much drama, saddened her. Taken from her care, she felt guilty they were abducted by that jerk.

A knock on her hospital door and Antonio walked in carrying flowers. "Hey, how are you feeling?"

"I'm good," she said, knowing she loved this man, fearful he remained angry with her. He had not been the same warm man who left her bed the morning after he was injured. "It's still painful but getting better. Tomorrow I'm going home, and my mother and sister will be taking care of me."

Oh. How she wanted him to kiss her and tell her everything was all right between them. Somehow she'd fallen in love with

Detective Dickhead and now she just wanted reassurances from him.

"Thanks for the flowers," she said. "This time I know they're from you."

A small smile filled his face. "Emma said to tell you to get well quick and hurry back to group."

Katherine's heart swelled with love and gratitude. Those kids held a special place in her heart and knew they had to be traumatized by what happened. Seeing their two friends taken from what they considered to be a safe place could leave damage.

"How's the investigation?"

"Everything is with the district attorney. We expect indictments soon, including one for Mr. Ray Castano, who owned the building where they operated. As the top guy in an organization involved in the sex trades, he's looking at prison time."

"That's great," Katherine said, relieved this investigation would finally be over.

"All the missing girls we found, including Madison Johnson. And no, Tomas was not the father of her child. He was trying to find out how much we knew. The ranch they used to fly the young women out when they were sold. The bordello here in Dallas was only for the most beautiful ladies until they wore them out."

"Disgusting," she said, wondering why he didn't kiss her when he came in the door.

Sinking down in a chair near her bed, he did not touch her.

"I owe you an apology," she said. "All the mean nasty things I said to you or called you were because I believed you were Emma's birth father. Until you said something to me, I had no idea you adopted her. That was wrong of me and I apologize."

Her words didn't seem to move him and that shocked her. Their relationship had changed and grown in the last few days and now he seemed to have withdrawn completely from her.

That scared her, because she loved Antonio and truly thought he was a wonderful man. The first man she ever considered marrying. And yet now a wall separated them that she didn't know how to overcome.

"Thank you for the apology. The name-calling didn't bother me. You never told me you were my daughter's counselor. Pat spoke to me at length about it, but I'm the kind of dad who wants to know everything about my daughter. You lied to me about a person I love."

A trickle of anger spiked through her. "No, I didn't lie. I just didn't tell you I was an intern counselor in your daughter's group sessions. Because of the Hippa laws, I couldn't."

"I should have been told," he said, and his emerald eyes darkened.

"Ashley said she mentioned Mateo in therapy. Is this true?"

Katherine frowned. "Until I was certain it was the same Mateo, I couldn't say anything. Shaggy was trying to find out for me. If I had known, you would've been the first person I told."

"But you didn't."

The man was angry at her, and in some ways, she couldn't blame him, but he had to understand her situation. She was bound by the law, and she could not talk about his daughter or any of the girls in the session.

"The problem is you take unnecessary chances. After I yelled at you to wait, we could have gone in together. But you insisted on charging Mateo and almost got Emma killed."

Dumbfounded, she watched him take a shaky breath. "That I would never forgive. You scare me. Never again, do I want to experience the kind of pain Emma and I went through when Sheila died."

Anger radiated from him. He was enraged she saved his daughter? That she risked her life because Emma had been kidnapped while at her group counseling.

The ache in her arm and shoulder slammed into her, but the biggest anguish centered around her heart.

"So you're upset with me because I didn't wait for you and your crippled leg to reach me, so we could charge Mateo together? Who would have had time to put Emma and Ashley in the car. Or would you have done it completely different?"

The man was screwed however he responded.

"All I'm saying is you take unnecessary chances. Dangerous moves that will someday get you killed."

"Answer my question."

"If I'd been well, I would never let you risk your life the way you did," he said. A frown crossed his face. "Your recklessness is too threatening. I buried one wife and I'm not going to bury another one. We can't be together."

For a moment, she just stared at him. "You're right, I'm reckless. I'm determined. I'm bullheaded and stubborn and loyal. Your daughter was taken during my counseling session, which made me responsible. Injured, you couldn't move around very well."

Tears welled up in her eyes, and she tried so hard to suppress them. "Because I understood how much you loved Emma, I risked everything to save her life."

Wiping the tears from her eyes, she took a deep breath. "Over the last week, you've helped me realize things about myself I need to work on, but here's somethings I don't need to change—my leadership, my determination, and my confidence.

"For the first time in my life, I've fallen in love, but right now all I feel is anger. If I had not stepped in, your daughter would be dead. But you're too blind to see that."

With a deep breath, she dug into her reserves of strength. "Maybe I wasn't wrong about you. The investigation is over, and I would never want to pose a risk to you or Emma. Get the hell out of my room and out of my life," she said, raising her voice and throwing the flowers at him. "You're still Detective Dickhead."

A sob escaped from her. Antonio's face turned red as he rose from the chair and walked out the door.

"Detective Dickhead!" she yelled, before sobs overwhelmed her.

For the first time in her life, she gave someone her heart, only to be told she was too careless. Well, screw him. What he didn't realize was that once she received her master's degree, she would no longer be a bounty hunter, but rather a counselor.

CHAPTER 40

Katherine lay curled on her side, her injured shoulder tucked into her body protectively. After spending all of yesterday crying, her eyes were red and swollen.

All her teenage life, she'd hated men. Hated what they did to women. Hated the fact her father left them to live a single's swinging life. Hated the man who got Nicole pregnant and deserted her. Now she hated she let herself become vulnerable. She had fallen in love with the dickhead and now he dumped her because she was too irresponsible.

His daughter's life had been at risk. The young girl he loved more than anything. And it was all Katherine's fault. What did he expect her to do? Sit back and paint her nails?

Men were so intimidated by her. But she could only be the person she was, and if they didn't love her this way, time to move on down the road.

A knock sounded at the door and her sister and mother came rushing in. "Time to go home."

Her mother stopped and looked at her. "What's wrong?"

What could she say? *My heart is broken. Detective Dickhead doesn't want me because I'm too reckless and I saved his Emma's life by almost losing my own?*

Tears welled up in her eyes and she sniffed. "Detective Dickhead said we're done. I'm too impetuous, dangerous, and I'm going to get someone killed."

"Katherine I've never seen you this way over a man," she said.

What? She wasn't supposed to fall in love. Just because she grew up hating men didn't mean that one would not eventually come along and steal her heart. But he didn't steal it; she gave him her love willingly and now she suffered.

"Well, now you have. Don't expect to see me like this again, because Detective Dickhead is the last man I'll love. No more. It hurts too much. You think you've gotten lucky and found someone who can put up with your craziness and instead you learn he's just a typical man."

Her sister came over and took her hand. "I'm sorry. He seemed like a nice guy. If anyone deserves happiness you do, Katherine. You're the one who has stood up and protected and fought for the three of us.

"Without you, my son would still be forced to see his deadbeat dad and I couldn't stand watching him drive away not knowing if they would return. Never paying his child support. You're the strongest woman I know and it's time for someone to stand up for you. What's his address, I'll go over there and kick his ass."

If she could hug her sister, she would have, but at the moment, no one touched her shoulder. The thought of Nicole kicking his ass brought a smile to her lips. "Thank you but leave him alone. He can't accept me the way I am, so time to move on."

Nicole frowned. "You are impetuous, even daring, but that's what makes you so good at what you do. Yes, I worry your impulsive nature will get you killed, but I also would not trust anyone else with my life or my son's. Because you would die protecting us and there is nothing more self-sacrificing."

Katherine stared up at her younger sister amazed at her. She didn't know Nicole felt that way about her. Sometimes she believed they weren't close, but to hear her say those words made her feel better.

"That means a lot, Nicole," Katherine said with a sigh. "So now I need to go on with life. Time to finish my master's degree and eventually I will leave the agency to go into counseling full time. Who needs Detective Dickhead if he can't appreciate me for who I am?"

Though her heart was still broken, her sister helped clear her mind of her doubts. No one would ever take away her right to protect the people she loved.

With a smile, her mother said, "Exactly. Now come on, let's help you dress, so we can sign the paperwork to walk out of this prison."

A grin crossed Katherine's face. "Yes, let's go home. And I'll try to be a better patient than last time, but I can't make any guarantees."

Laughter came from her mother. "Dear, all your life you were the child that kept me on my toes and worried me at night. Even now."

"Sorry, Mom," she said and sat up on the side of the bed. Time to move on and forget about the handsome detective she had fallen in love with. No more.

CHAPTER 41

A month later Katherine was in the bathroom hanging over the toilet retching her guts up. With every spasm, she hated Detective Dickhead more. Finally, she finished, rinsed out her mouth and washed her hands as she gazed at herself in the mirror. Of all the luck. Outside she could hear whispers.

With a yank of the door, she startled everyone who stood waiting for her. The entire office stared at her, their faces stunned. She felt that way as well after she peed on the stick and the plus sign appeared. Dear God!

"Yes, that's right I'm pregnant and you're all sworn to secrecy. Do you understand me? No one tells him unless they want to spend grueling hours in the labor room with me."

That should be a threat worthy of them keeping their mouths shut.

"Now, honey, don't you think he deserves to be told? You hate men who abandon their children."

It was true, but when he left, she didn't realize she was pregnant.

"You're right, I do, so this one will not have the chance. He can't walk away from this child because he's never going to learn the baby is his. Are we clear?"

"That's not fair to the father," Gina said.

One of her goals was to clean up her mouth, so she didn't say her first thoughts. Otherwise, Gina would be hearing a string of f-bombs about what she considered fair for Antonio.

"Do you think I care about the father right now? He's already a baby daddy because he walked away from me. End of discussion."

Tears welled up in her eyes as she turned and hurried toward her safe haven, her office. In almost five weeks, she hadn't seen Antonio, and she never had to see him again.

Jennifer followed her, her slightly rounded stomach showing the progression of her pregnancy. "Are you all right?"

How did you answer when your heart had been rejected and the consequences of your actions would arrive in about eight months?

"Other than morning sickness, sore breasts, and the incredible need to pee all the time, I'm fine," she said. "After going through surgery, when I realized I was pregnant, I was terrified, but the doctor assured me the baby is okay. We're going to do an ultrasound in another month and possibly an amniotic fluid test."

"How far along were you when the shooting occurred?"

"Less than a week," she said. "The first time we made love, the condom broke. At the time, I wasn't worried.

"Nothing is going to change in my life. I'm still going to finish school, work here, and..."

As much as she tried to hold her emotions in check, sometimes the tears just flowed. Damn pregnancy hormones and heartache.

Tears rolled down her cheek. "I never thought this would happen to me. I made a vow to never be unmarried and pregnant, especially after my sister. And now look at me."

"You loved him. This baby is a result of your love," Jennifer said.

And that was why she didn't want Antonio to know. He left, but now she had her sweet peanut. The outcome of their time together.

"Promise me you won't tell him. If he doesn't want me, then he doesn't get the baby either. This is my child now. No one else's."

Jennifer sighed. "Honey, I wish it was that easy. But as the father, he has rights. I'll honor your decision, but you should tell him."

To hell with his rights. As far as she was concerned, this sweet peanut belonged to her.

"Detective Dickhead doesn't deserve anything. I'm afraid he'll tell the judge I'm dangerous. I'm impulsive and reckless and I'll kill this child, and you and I know that's not true. Right now, I would give my life for this child, and he or she is a mere speck inside my womb."

That was her biggest fear, he would try to take the child from her once he learned of her pregnancy. With his background in law enforcement, he had a lot of contacts, and she could see some judge giving the baby to him. She would never allow that to happen.

"Isn't it funny how quickly you fall in love with that tiny little bean," Jennifer said. "We're creating another generation of Lipstick and Lead."

Katherine stared at her. "You're right. We are. As much as I talk bad about Antonio, I still love him and probably always will."

CHAPTER 42

*A*ntonio felt like a monster. One moment he was raging at someone and the next sad. His loneliness seemed to have compounded over the last month and now he noticed couples everywhere. The world belonged to couples. With him the lone outsider looking in.

Even his daughter couldn't seem to help him overcome this sadness that refused to go away.

After Sheila died, he'd been overwrought with grief and loneliness, but this experience was different. Inside his brain, a war raged. One side said he was the biggest fool on the planet and the other side said he had done what was best for everyone.

Katherine would never fit into his and Emma's world. Before the relationship became serious, he had ended it. Yet why did everything feel out of kilter, like he took a wrong turn down a dead-end street?

"Dad," Emma said, sitting across from him at the dinner table. "Once again, you're spaced out."

Emma had been complaining since the shooting he had been distant, mean, and surly.

"Are you all right? You're not your normal self. Maybe you should see a counselor."

"No," he said, thinking he didn't want to cross paths with Katherine again for a long, long time. It would be like ripping his bullet wound open and pouring hot acid on the skin.

"Katherine announced today she's no longer going to be leading our sessions."

"What?" he asked, surprised she would quit.

"Said she is going to focus on school and preparing to take her final exams."

"Oh," he said and thought how weird because she had been doing the counseling and Lipstick and Lead and going to school. What changed?

"When she rescued me and you were so upset, I hoped there might be something between the two of you," Emma said. "Was there?"

God, his daughter was too smart. Emma was growing up and noticing the way men and women acted toward one another. "Yes, we liked each other, but she's too careless. She could have gotten you killed."

Emma's eyes grew wide, and she stared at him in shock. "What? Honestly, you believe that? Dad, she saved my life. Mateo had pulled the trigger and said to me, *pray, you're dead.* If not for her, I would not be here."

Wow, that piece of the puzzle he didn't know, but it did tell him he would not have arrived in time to save Emma. But still, that didn't change things. Someday because of her rashness, her impulsiveness, Katherine would die.

"That still doesn't change the fact her lack of discipline will get her killed. And I can't go through someone else I care about dying."

With a shake of her head, his daughter said frustrated, "Go to counseling."

"What does that mean?"

"After mother died, I would lie awake at night, worrying something would happen to you. You are still on the force. Just like Mom, you work dangerous cases.

"We talked about it in group. Katherine told me walking across the street or a car accident or even a heart attack could take you in an instant. No one is guaranteed a long life. We need to enjoy the moments spent together, even the bad ones, and realize this could all end in a second."

Staring across the table at Emma, he felt proud. What a brilliant child she was becoming, and he couldn't help but think Katherine helped make her into this person. Because her counseling sessions taught his daughter to accept what life threw at her and not let anything ruin her.

What she said was true, but the pain of loss was gut wrenching. Yet what was he going through now? Though he ended the relationship, he missed her every minute of the day. How many times did he look up thinking he heard her laugh?

"Have I told you how proud I am of you? You're becoming an amazing young woman."

"Talk to her, Dad. At least end this animosity between you."

"Animosity?"

Emma smiled. "Let's just say she refused to speak to me about you. She's never refused to speak to me about anything, but you are an off-limits private discussion. I can bring you up in group, but not personal stuff about the two of you."

So the counselor, Katherine, had put boundaries in place. That was interesting.

"Did you love her?"

Now that hit low when his own daughter recognized his emotions were involved and knew he wouldn't lie to her.

"Yes, but I can't be with her because I don't want to go through losing someone like I did with your mother."

"Then don't," she said. "Be alone the rest of your life and never be willing to find someone who makes you happy."

His too-smart-for-her-own-good daughter got up from the table and started to clean the dishes. Leaving him to think once more.

Was he afraid? Hell, yes, he was terrified. Was it because of the danger they experienced each day? Of course. But was it better to live by himself? To miss out on her funny expressions, her way of putting someone in their place. The way she laughed, smiled and gave him hell.

What about her reckless behavior? Could he live with the thought any day might be her last?

No, he didn't want to be without her another day. Damn, he had made a huge mistake and now he worried if she would forgive him.

Suddenly he rose and glanced at his watch. Five o'clock. The Lipstick and Lead agency would be closing soon, but she often worked late.

"You want to go with me?"

"Where are you going?" she asked, putting her dishes in the dishwasher.

"To the Lipstick and Lead agency to see Katherine."

Emma swirled toward him and smiled. "Yes. Let's go."

"Would you be all right if I asked her to marry me?"

"Finally, I thought you would never ask. Yes, I can't wait."

Some days Emma was smarter than her father.

CHAPTER 43

Katherine stood and leaned back, stretching her back. It was late and only a few remained at the agency. With the pregnancy, her energy level was next to nothing, and she needed her rest.

With a sigh, she shut down her computer and started to clean her desk off. Since the breakup, she hated going home to her apartment. It seemed like a lonely place now.

But soon, she would have a baby and all the equipment filling the small space. Life would be different, but she was determined not to let this child change her direction in life.

The outside door opened, but she didn't pay any mind, though the noise in the office escalated. As she finished packing up for the night, she picked up her purse to head out.

The door to her office opened and there stood Antonio.

"What are you doing here?" she asked, fear scurrying up her spine. Had someone told him about the baby? If she ever learned who spilled her secrets, she would kill them.

"Look, sometimes I'm not the smartest man on the planet. That night I was so afraid for Emma. At the time, I blamed you for her kidnapping. Then to see the woman I love sacrificing herself to save my daughter, I feared I would lose both of you.

"Panic, like I never felt before overwhelmed me. I've already lost one woman to a bullet and the fear of losing a second one made me into a raving lunatic."

She started to say something, and he held up his hand.

"In the last month, I've been miserable. I missed you. Your laughter, your smart-ass attitude, your funny quips, the way you keep me on my toes and just how being with you makes me happy. When we began working together, I believed I hated you, but how quickly I realized that actually I love you. Can't live without you and want to spend whatever time we have left on this earth together."

Tears welled up in Katherine's eyes. Could she forgive him for walking out and leaving her heart broken at the hospital?

He dropped to one knee and opened a square box. "I'm serious. On the way here, I stopped and bought a wedding ring. Whether we're married for one week or fifty years, I want you by my side as my wife."

This was the man she loved, and she could forgive him of just about anything. She pulled him up, her heart hammering in her chest. "Can you live with my impulsive, reckless ways?"

"Yes, I want all of you, the way you are. No changing for me or anyone else. I love you for being the reckless, impulsive person you are, Katherine. Please marry me."

"Yes," she said breathlessly, before she layered her lips across his, kissing him, joy filling her that finally she had the love she wanted. Her own baby daddy...

Suddenly she leaned back in his arms. "No more secrets between us, ever. So there are a couple of things you need to know. As soon as I graduate, I'm leaving Lipstick and Lead."

Relief spread like a smile on his face, and she thought, but that's not all.

"And the night the condom broke...well, you're going to be a father again."

The shock that crossed his face, made her laugh. "Really? You're expecting?"

"Yes, the doctor confirmed it."

"Why didn't you call me?"

Like that would have happened. A smile spread across her face.

"Because Detective Baby Daddy, you walked away before I learned the truth. But now, promise me that through sickness and health, diapers and feedings, you'll be by my side forever and never walk away from me and our baby."

"No way you're getting rid of me. I love you, Katherine McKenzie. And we're having a baby."

A happy laugh escaped her, and they heard the others out in the office clapping and turned to witness them standing outside the window watching them celebrate their happiness.

CHAPTER 44

Two months later, the newlyweds and Emma gathered in the doctor's office. Today Katherine received her first sonogram, and they would soon learn the sex of the baby. They were all nervous and excited as the technician rubbed the gel over Katherine's swelling stomach.

"How many weeks along are you?" the lady asked.

"Twelve weeks," she confirmed, knowing her waist was rapidly expanding.

The technician frowned and Katherine worried something was wrong with the baby. This had been her biggest concern that the surgery, the anesthesia, might have harmed their little peanut, even though the doctor kept telling her everything was fine.

What if it wasn't?

"Look right there. That is a boy," she said. Suddenly she stopped and went back over another area and Katherine saw it on the ultrasound.

Her heart leaped out of her chest and started pounding furiously. No, that couldn't be.

"Oh my God," she said as the second baby appeared to wave.

"Congratulations, Mr. and Mrs. Marino, you're having twins. Baby one is a boy and baby two is a girl."

Emma squealed and jumped up and down, thrilled. "Twins."

Antonio looked at her and then shook his head. "Damn, you just had to be an overachiever didn't you."

She laughed. "Don't forget you promised to love me during diaper changes and bottle feedings."

He reached down and kissed her. "Double trouble. I love you, Katherine."

"Love you too, but next time we're using two condoms."

THANKS FOR READING! I loved these two characters probably the most of this series and they needed twins. I hope you enjoyed them as well. Please be sure to leave a review. It helps authors sell more books.

PLEASE LEAVE A REVIEW

Did you enjoy the book? Reviews help authors. I would appreciate you posting a review.

Follow Sylvia McDaniel on Facebook.
http://facebook.com/SylviaMcDanielAuthor

Sign up for my New Book Alert at www.SylviaMcDaniel.com and receive a complimentary book.

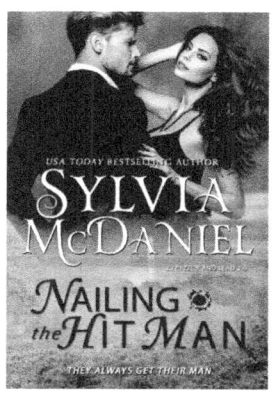

The Redhead with the Gun Won't be Denied

Jennifer McKenzie Delgado along with her cousins own the fourth generation of Lipstick and Lead. Together, they are determined their business of bounty hunting will continue. The problem is they hold a million-dollar bond on a bail jumper who is nowhere to be found. With the bond in default, they have ten days before the money is due and they lose the company.

Once again, Carson Lopez is mistaken for his criminal twin, Christopher, but this time by a beautiful, sexy, bounty hunter. Also searching for his sibling, he wants answers why his brother is killing off Family members. With Jennifer posing as his girlfriend, Carson flies to Vegas to confront his brother.

When she becomes the target of the hit man, it's all Carson can do to keep the redhead from being the bull's eye. But with her company on the line, Jennifer will take any risk to get her man. Including losing the one she's come to love to organized crime.

Get Your Copy At Your Favorite Retailer!

Will the Bounty Hunter Catch the Billionaire?

Brittany McKenzie, ex-military sniper, comes from a long line of bounty hunters. The night her cousin Jennifer marries, she has a one-night stand with a gorgeous unknown man who piques her interest. Back at work when she goes on her next assignment, she can't believe his face stares back at her.

Billionaire Mark Davis has been framed for embezzlement and is determined to clear his name. The only obstacle is the blonde bounty hunter, who he spent one glorious night in Vegas with, doesn't care what he thinks. Can he convince her of his innocence?

Will the sharp-shooter and the billionaire discover who is destroying his reputation and will the heat they ignited in Vegas continue to burn?

Get Your Copy at Your Favorite Retailer

Also By Sylvia McDaniel
Contemporary Romance
Return to Cupid, Texas
Cupid Stupid
Cupid Scores
Cupid's Dance
Cupid Help Me!
Cupid Cures
**Cupid's Heart
Cupid Santa
**Cupid Second Chance
Cupid Charmer
Return to Cupid Box Set Books 1-3
Return to Cupid Box Set Books 4-6

Contemporary Romance
My Sister's Boyfriend
The Wanted Bride
The Reluctant Santa
The Relationship Coach
Secrets, Lies, & Online Dating

Bride, Texas Multi-Author Series
**The Unlucky Bride

Lipstick and Lead 2.0
Nailing the Hit Man
Nailing the Billionaire
Nailing the Single Dad

The Langley Legacy
Collin's Challenge

ALSO BY

Short Sexy Reads
Racy Reunions Series
Paying For the Past
Her Christmas Lie
Cupid's Revenge

Western Historicals
A Hero's Heart
Second Chance Cowboy
Ethan

American Brides
**Katie: Bride of Virginia

Angel Creek Christmas Brides
**Charity
**Ginger
**Minne
**Cora

Bad Girls of the West
Scandalous Sadie
Ravenous Rose
Tempting Tessa
Nellie's Redemption

The Burnett Brides Series
The Rancher Takes A Bride
The Outlaw Takes A Bride
The Marshal Takes A Bride
The Christmas Bride
Boxed Set

Lipstick and Lead Series

ALSO BY

Desperate
Deadly
Dangerous
Daring
**Determined
Deceived
Defiant
Devious
Lipstick and Lead Box Set Books 1-4
Lipstick and Lead Box Set Books 5-9
Lipstick and Lead Box Set Books 1-9
**Quinlan's Quest

Mail Order Bride Tales
**A Brother's Betrayal
**Pearl
**Ace's Bride

Scandalous Suffragettes of the West
**Abigail
Bella
Mistletoe Scandal

Southern Historical Romance
A Scarlet Bride

The Cuvier Women
Wronged
Betrayed
Beguiled
Boxed Set

The Debutante's of Durango
The Debutante's Scandal

ALSO BY

The Debutante's Gamble
The Debutante's Revenge
The Debutante's Santa

** **Denotes a sweet book.**

Want to learn about my new releases before anyone else? Sign up for my New Book Alert and receive a complimentary book.

USA Today Best-selling author, Sylvia McDaniel obviously has too much time on her hands. With over seventy western historical and contemporary romance novels, she spends most days torturing her characters. Bad boys deserve punishment and even good girls get into trouble. Always looking for the next plot twist, she's known for her sweet, funny, family-oriented romances.

Married to her best friend for over twenty-five years, they recently moved to the state of Colorado where they like to hike, and enjoy the beauty of the forest behind their home with their spoiled dachshund Zeus. (He has his own column in her newsletter.)

Their grown son, still lives in Texas. An avid football watcher, she loves the Broncos and the Cowboys, especially when they're winning.

www.SylviaMcDaniel.com
Sylvia@SylviaMcDaniel.com
The End!

Made in United States
Orlando, FL
30 May 2025